D0735937

BISON
BOOKS

FLYOVER FICTION

Series editor: Ron Hansen

IN
REACH

Pamela Carter Joern

University of Nebraska Press

Lincoln and London

Library of Congress Cataloging-in-Publication Data
Joern, Pamela Carter, 1948–
[Short stories. Selections]
In reach / Pamela Carter Joern.
pages   cm—(Flyover fiction)
ISBN 978-0-8032-5483-1 (pbk.: alk. paper)
ISBN 978-0-8032-5676-7 (pdf)
ISBN 978-0-8032-5677-4 (epub)
ISBN 978-0-8032-5678-1 (mobi)
1. Nebraska—Fiction. 2. Domestic fiction. I. Title.
PS3610.025A6 2014
813'.6—dc23   2014001283

Set in Scala OT by Renni Johnson.
Designed by Ashley Muehlbauer.

For Shannon and Raegan, with love and admiration

R E A C H (rēch) n. an unbroken expanse of land or water
<a *reach* of open prairie>

The founder of Reach, Nebraska, was a British immigrant named Arthur Weston. Weston had grown up on the shores of Kent and made his way to America as an orphan aboard the *Queen Mary* in 1851. He homesteaded in the North Platte River valley, and when he saw the wide expanse of prairie grass undulating in the breeze, he said it reminded him of the open reach of the ocean.

CONTENTS

ACKNOWLEDGMENTS

"So this is Nebraska," Ted Kooser writes in a poem. Not being a poet, I set out to capture Nebraska in these stories. Of course, as is the nature of fiction, none of these stories happened. Out of a flash of memory here, an intriguing shadow there, I followed a path of wonder to see what it would reveal to me. This may not be your Nebraska, but it is mine, mingled with all the places I have been since, all the loves and losses I have known, all the thoughts that have crossed my mind, and all the dragonflies and sunflowers and prairie grasses that worked their enchantments on me. My intention is to pay tribute to the beauty and complexities of lives lived hard and well. To the people who did and still do make up the world of the western plains, thank you.

This collection of stories was a long time in the making. Short of thanking the entire universe and at the risk of leaving someone out, I want to express my gratitude to the following: Sheila O'Connor and Mary Rockcastle, my mentors in the Hamline MFA program where some of these stories germinated; Mary Bednarowski, who read the most recent stories and never failed to believe in them; the writers' group from Mallard Island; my Hamline writing buddies; the staff and my students at the Loft Literary Center, who inspire me with their dedication and love of writing; Kristen

Elias Rowley, Kathryn Owens, Julie Gutin, and their colleagues at University of Nebraska Press, who have so beautifully offered my work to the reading public; our Judson Church community and all our friends, near and far, who have supported not only my writing, but also the life it engenders. Last, but never least, I wish to thank my family: my mother and my late mother-in-law, both longtime residents of small towns in Nebraska; my Aunt Dot and Uncle Ken, who have been waiting for this book; my aunts, uncles, and cousins who fanned out from Nebraska but never forgot the family ties; Bob and Norma, Kent and Leania, Linda and Bruce, Gayle and Jim, Don, my nieces and nephews and their children; my daughters and their husbands, Shannon and Matt, Raegan and Jacob; my own Fab Four—Nadine, Elijah, Henry, and Tyson—who remind me that life demands attention; and to Brad, for all and everything.

Some of these stories were published elsewhere, and I am grateful to the editors who chose them. Three of them were published by *Minnesota Monthly* magazine: "Confessions" (Tamarack Award winner), November 2001; "Running in Place" (Tamarack Award finalist), January 2006; and "Fire on His Mind," under the title "The Fireman" (Tamarack Award winner), November 2008. "Judgment Day" appeared in the Summer 2003 issue of the *Red Rock Review*; "After Death" in the *South Dakota Review*, Summer 2004; and "Lessons at the PO" in the *Great River Review*, Spring 2009.

IN REACH

RUNNING IN PLACE

Wayne McManus sits at the hospital bedside of his dying cousin. He's reading Mary Oliver poems aloud, the poet lying on her stomach, studying a single blade of grass, a grasshopper's wings. His own spindly legs are crossed knee over knee, bony silk-socked ankles nested in black wing-tipped shoes polished to mirror the sky, the laces new and waxy. His blue dress shirt snugs into the waistband of gray pleated trousers, belted with Italian leather. Glasses in small metal frames pinch a narrow nose, his eyes an icy blue. Blond hair, trimmed and tidy, shot through with gray. He looks like a character from *Masterpiece Theatre*, not a bank teller who's lived all his life (save one indescribable summer) in Reach, Nebraska.

The body on the bed shifts. The younger man is quiet now, morphine dripping into his arm, his skin translucent. Wayne has read about that. The lesions, too. One high on Mark's forehead, another on his arm. Wayne helped the nurse turn him once. Put his hands under Mark's body and lifted him while she tugged on the stained sheet. It was like lifting a skeleton, the bones loose and jangling. He feared that some part of Mark would break off, his leg, say, or a brittle arm that would shatter on the floor to be swept up by Hazel, the scowling cleaning woman.

Mark strains to raise his head. Wayne lays the book of poetry, open and pages down, on the bedside table. The room smells of antiseptic, the walls white and sterile, but as he leans over Mark, his nostrils twitch at the foul odor emanating from Mark's mouth.

"Do you want water?" Wayne asks.

Mark shakes his head. "What's that?" he says, his voice whispery and coarse.

"Water?" Wayne repeats.

Mark rolls his head toward the book. "No, that."

"Mary Oliver," Wayne says. Then, quoting from the poet, "'Tell me, what is it you plan to do with your one wild and precious life?'"

"I like Bond," Mark says.

"Bond?"

"James Bond."

"Oh, dear," Wayne says.

What do they have in common, really? Mark's lived in San Francisco. He once personally met Jerry Garcia. Except for an occasional Christmas card, Wayne hasn't heard from him in twenty years. He only found out that Mark was sick because Maude, the hospital receptionist, called him.

Back at the bank, through a small window, Wayne smiles at his customers (he knows them all by name) and counts out tens, twenties, hundreds, bills creased and soiled from human hands. He wears gloves.

Later, inside his house, he walks past leather upholstery, cases of books, watercolor paintings to a back bedroom where his hand slides along a pebbly plaster wall, flips a switch that lights 150 hurricane lamps crowded on shelves lining the room. More than half have been electrified, but the other 63, with their original oil wicks intact, are illuminated by lights recessed within the shelves. The lamps displayed here are his current favorites. Another 450 are boxed and labeled and tucked away in his basement. He runs his hand over the pink roses, the delicate fluted edges, hand-painted globes of exquisite little worlds.

After supper (a meal of cold turkey and salad), he dons a light jacket to ward off the October chill and walks three blocks to the Albertsons' house. He raps lightly on the door, stands patiently while Mary looks through the peephole. She lets him in, stands there in her black lace-up shoes, a gray crepe dress, her white hair mashed under a net. Her back is stooped, the only real change in her since she taught his fifth-grade class fifty-three years ago. Propped in an overstuffed chair, her brother Dave's arms rest on long-necked swans crocheted into doilies, a needlepoint pillow of pansies behind his head. He doesn't rise or speak when Wayne steps in. Wayne sits forward on the edge of the Edwardian couch, signaling that he won't stay long.

"How's business?" Dave asks. The tube to Dave's oxygen tank snakes across the floor, his breathing shallow and labored.

"Not the same without you," Wayne says, though Dave has been retired from the bank for twelve years.

Mary seats herself in the rocking chair, pulls her knitting into her lap. Heavy brocade curtains veil the windows, the room spiked with shadows. No television, of course. A lamp with fringed shade. Antique tables, hand-carved. An oil painting grown dark with age, a bucolic landscape, sheep on hillsides, far from the Nebraska prairie. There's nothing of tumbleweeds or windmills in this room. Wayne wonders, as he always does, what they do all day. They don't allow any other visitors. Their groceries are delivered from the Jack & Jill to their back door. After the boy has gone, Mary retrieves the bags from the back porch. If they're too heavy, she waits for Wayne and asks if he will carry them to her kitchen counter.

Wayne first came here because Dave told him they had an old kerosene lamp that had belonged to their mother. The top globe broken. Worthless, Dave said. Wayne asked if he could take a look at it, and when he did, he could hardly conceal his excitement. Some unknown but gifted artist had painted a picnic by a river, two laughing young men against a backdrop of shimmering yellow and autumn gold. One extended his hand toward the other. Apart from them, seated on the ground, a woman wearing white clutched a parasol and looked off across the river, her face invisible. He bought it from them for $15.00. He took it to an antiques restorer down by Ogallala and had a top globe hand-made, painted with sky to make a roof over this perfect world. Whenever Mary asks about her mother's lamp, he lies to her. *Not much could be done. Packed away in my basement.* Because he lies, he mows their lawn in the summer. Lights the pilot light on the furnace in the winter. When they need to go to the doctor in Scottsbluff, he drives them.

"Any news?" Mary asks.

Wayne clasps his hands, clears his throat. "My cousin Mark is in the hospital."

"Wilhelmina's grandson?" Mary says.

Wayne nods. "Truman's boy."

Mary knits a row. She's making socks, narrow cotton yarn, gray. She'll wear them herself, bunched around her ankles above low-heeled shoes.

"Truman was in my class," she says.

Wayne nods again.

"Not much of a thinker," she says.

Wayne bristles and, at the same time, can't fathom himself. Why should he, of all people, want to stick up for Tru?

"Mark's dying," Wayne says, to punish her a little.

Mary's needles stop for a fraction of a second. He waits for her to ask him why. He's decided he will say that it is cancer, which it is, by now. But she doesn't ask. She goes on knitting.

Back in his living room, it's only 8:00 p.m. Not enough time used up. He pours himself a glass of red wine, settles into his leather recliner, adjusts the lamp, and lifts a book. He finds that he can't concentrate, thinking instead that Mary could be a mean teacher, batting the backs of hands with rulers, raising red welts on knuckles, making big dumb kids—like Tru—cry out in pain.

Wayne continues to sit with Mark. Every day when he enters the hospital room, he has to fight the urge to remove his shoes. Some old vestige of what one is supposed to do on holy ground, like Moses in the wilderness. He would not be surprised if the bed burst into flames. He keeps reading poetry, Whitman, even Yeats, trying to understand what is happening. When he is sure no nurse will come barging into the room, he speaks in gentle tones. "It's all right," he says, though clearly, it is not all right.

He wants to know—things. What's it like? Love?

Sometimes Mark looks at him and speaks. "Where's my momma?"

"She died. With your daddy, in that old truck. You remember. You were seven years old."

"I want my momma." Later, "Where's Curtis?"

Wayne scoots his chair close to the bed, bends his lips to Mark's ear. "Tell me about Curtis," he says. He wants to hear of candlelight, whispered words, limbs entwined, taut skin sliding.

"Momma?" Mark says.

"Shhh. Quiet, now. Momma wants you to rest."

At night, he thinks about that summer in Denver. Was that love? How could something that moved him so far outside himself be good for him? He came out of the two months he spent there like someone surfacing from a fever, dazed and disoriented. One morning, he woke and turned his head in the dim light of a hotel room. He heard sounds in the bathroom, smelled the heavy odors of sweat and semen. His glance fell on a naked light bulb dangling from the ceiling, a pair of pants thrown over the back of a chair, a cracked window repaired with yellowed tape. Before a thought could form in his head, he'd slipped on his shoes. I don't know you, he was thinking, as his feet trod down the stairs. He tripped on the bottom step, something he would recall for years. He would relive the sharp stab in his ankle, but he would not remember the color of eyes or shape of jaw or the tremble in his own hand.

On the day Mark slips into the final coma, he whispers a few words to Wayne. Wayne bends low to hear them.

"I never wanted—I never wanted . . ." Mark stops, gasps for air.

"It's okay," Wayne says. What does the past matter? Truman nearly beat him to death, tied him to a barbed wire fence with his pants down around his ankles. None of that was Mark's fault. The boy wasn't even born yet. Don't apologize for that sorry sonofabitch, Wayne wants to say. But all he can manage is, "It's okay."

"I never wanted—" Mark grasps him by the shirtfront, pulls him down to the bed. "To be like you," he says.

Afraid that he will start to cry, Wayne only nods. He understands completely. Who would choose this? He melts with gratitude. Transparent and relieved, like listening to Bach, his soul wrung out and connected and momentarily not alone.

"I never wanted"—Mark's hand still clenches the starched front of Wayne's shirt—"to be afraid. Like you."

Wayne steps back. He raises his hand to quell the sting, as if he's been slapped, thinks of a string of retorts—he's not the one who ran away—but before he can shape his lips around his defense, Mark slides under, like someone who's fallen through ice, and though Wayne comes every day and sits longer hours, though he holds Mark in his arms through the final shudder into death, Mark doesn't waken.

He attends Mark's funeral, although Wilhelmina will not look at him. He does not sit with her. He stands in the back at the cemetery, not under the tarp that protects Wilhelmina and her friends from the November wind. She did not visit her grandson in the hospital; he knows that for a fact. She neither forgets nor forgives, and while he stares at her stiffened back, a flock of geese rises from the river a half mile north and honks across the sky.

Two days later, Wayne is fired from his job at the bank. The banker's son has taken over, moved back to Reach after Harvard and years of failure on the New York Stock Exchange. He cites change, more automation, redundancy. Wayne doesn't even have a desk to clean out.

He doesn't tell Mary and Dave for another week. He doesn't want them to connect the loss of his job to Mark's funeral, to the fact that Wilhelmina has all the money from the sale of her ranch in that bank.

He's sitting in their living room, under the rosy glow of the lamp, when he lets them know that he's decided to retire.

"Oh?" Mary says. She rests her knitting in her lap.

"Why?" Dave says. He rallies to ask this question, piercing eyes, then sinks back.

"Time to do other things," Wayne says, his voice upbeat and cheerful.

They lapse into silence. Dave falls asleep, a thin line of drool spinning from the corner of his mouth to the needlepoint pillow. It must be filthy, that pillow, and Wayne reminds himself not to touch it. Mary resumes knitting, the click-click of the needles twanging Wayne's nerves. He rubs his forehead with his hand. He despises people who have their hands on themselves all the time, grooming a mustache, pulling their ears, pushing their glasses up on their nose. He's pondering the larger fate of humanity, how eventually we all become what we detest, when Mary speaks.

"Have I told you about this ring on my left hand?" she asks.

Wayne shakes his head. He has wondered. A big diamond ring. An inheritance, he supposed. He's heard that there was family money. This high-quality furniture came from somewhere.

"I was engaged," she says.

"Really?"

"I was young, once." Her sharp tone. That teacher voice that made kids not like her. He shouldn't have acted so surprised.

"It was during the war," she says. "I lived in Cheyenne, then. I was teaching school and living in a boardinghouse. I met him through mutual friends."

"The war separated you?"

"We had one last evening. I had decided to break it off. I loved him, but something was missing."

"So, did you?"

"We had dinner at the Plains Hotel. We drank wine and laughed. He was a lovely man, curly dark hair."

She stops to adjust her knitting, gather her thoughts. Wayne says nothing. He's working hard to picture Mary young, with a man, drinking wine.

"He walked me back to my hotel. I tried to work up the courage to tell him, and then in the lobby, he took both my hands in his. There was another young couple kissing in front of the elevator. She wore a green hat with three white feathers and a rhinestone ornament. I was thinking how fine I'd look in that hat when he said, 'Mary, I have to tell you something. I love you, but I am not in love with you. I don't think I'll ever be in love with a woman.'"

Wayne's hands go numb. He fights the urge to curl his arms across his chest. Hide, hide, rings in his head, but there's nowhere to go. He shifts his weight to stand, when her voice goes on.

"He told me to keep this ring. He said, 'When you wear it, remember that I love you.' I didn't know what to tell our families and friends, so I said nothing. He was killed at Normandy."

Wayne waits, but she has stopped talking.

"Lucky he died," Wayne says. He cannot keep the bitterness out of his voice.

"Do you think so?" She doesn't look up. Her fingers slide along the needle, counting stitches.

Three weeks after he's been fired, halfway into December, Wayne decides to go to Denver for the weekend. He packs a small suitcase and drives south.

The air is heavy and dull, an anvil-colored sky that presses on the plains. Feeling low, he stops in Kimball at a truck stop. A bell attached to the diner door clangs when he opens it. A tired waitress looks up from behind the counter. She's white-headed, heavyset, wearing glasses. He's seen a million like her. He picks out a booth along the outside wall and runs his hand along the underside of the table, checking for fresh wads of gum before he sits, having once ruined a good pair of pants.

The waitress brings him a steaming cup of coffee, a murky film skimming the top. He orders a plate of eggs and bacon, why not? Patsy Cline sings mournfully in the background, amid static. Gray outside. Puddles of muck and dirty boot prints on the floor.

Wayne sips his coffee and looks around. In one corner, a woman huddles in a brown coat, leafing through a stack of bills piled in front of her. Occasionally, she tugs at her hair, then back to fingering the envelopes. A trucker sits at the counter, beefy hands cradling a coffee cup, eyes bloodshot and glazed with road hypnosis, an inch of hairy skin revealed by low-slung jeans. A teenager (shouldn't she be in school?) occupies the adjacent booth, her back against the window, legs slung up on the seat. Heavy mascara fringes her eyes, black blobs gummed on the lash tips, her lips red as an overripe plum. The aging waitress brings her a cup of coffee, a carton of half-and-half in her other hand. She stands and creams the coffee for the girl, then walks away. There's a dog, too, lying on the floor, a black Lab with one foot missing.

Wayne lets out a long breath and slides into a strange, unsettling calm. He knows these people, even the dog. The way they leave the radio on at night to trick themselves into thinking someone else is in the room. The stickiness of spilled syrup, left to dry on the kitchen counter. The sweating hands when they check the mail, the answering machine. Ask them, any one of them, who's waiting for you at home? He knows the answer. Like him, they find rest in these gray walls, the broke down look of this place, the knowledge that people come and go, come and go, nobody stays, because this isn't supposed to be home. Nobody pretends that they belong. Here, where everyone is transient and anonymous, nobody betrays you.

He stays as long as he can without drawing attention to himself. Eventually, he tears himself away, gets in his car, and stops at the top of the driveway, unable to decide what to do. He can't show his face in Reach, the whole town buzzing over his loss of job. If he goes on to Denver, he could get a fresh start, but does he even know where to begin? It won't be any different in Denver than it is in Reach. Everywhere he goes, he takes his damn self, and for him, the likes of him, there is no coming home.

When he hears the knock on his window, he mistakes it for a gunshot. He feels for the wound, his hand moving around on his chest, the pain real, searing, and then he hears a man's voice.

"You all right in there?"

He rolls the foggy window down a few inches and leans back to peer out. It's the trucker from the diner, a leather jacket thrown over his plaid flannel shirt, a toothpick riding his lower lip. Snot dribbles from his nose, and the man wipes at it with the back of his hand. "You been sitting there a while. Everything okay?"

"Fine," Wayne says.

"You goin' to Denver?"

"I thought about it."

"Because that kid over there wants a ride."

The man hitches his thumb toward the teenager hunched by the diner's front door. It's the girl from inside. She looks mad as hell and scared, her eyes glassy. She's on something, meth probably, these kids today.

"You can't take her?" Wayne says.

"Nah. I'm headed to Sidney, to Cabela's. She asked me, but I ain't goin' that direction."

The girl sees them talking about her. She looks down, scuffs her feet, then turns and disappears back inside the diner. She's standing in the outer foyer, between the gumball machine and a bulletin board with tacked-up notices of garage sales. Through the window, they can see she's pulled out a cell phone.

"Probably had a fight with her boyfriend," the trucker says.

"Or her parents," Wayne offers.

"Yeah."

The girl is gesturing wildly, her fingers splayed, hands tense. She whirls around. The two men watch her and don't speak, and finally, she cries with heaving sobs, her head propped against the window.

"Well, I guess she'll be all right, then," the trucker says.

"I suppose." Wayne knows what the man is thinking. Someone is on the other end of that phone line.

"Well," the man says, looking toward his truck.

"Go ahead," Wayne says. "I'll wait."

The man nods. He moves away, and without turning his head, lifts his hand behind him in a farewell wave.

Wayne sits in his car, engine running, for what seems like a long time. The girl has snapped her phone together and stands in the entryway, eyes dark and watching. A beat-up Chevy pulls into the parking lot, one fender bent like a potato chip. The driver is a woman, middle-aged, her hair a frowsy mess. Without bothering to turn off the car or close the door behind her, she catapults inside the diner. He watches her fold the girl in her arms, pat her on the back. The girl is taller than the woman, but she manages to slump down, turn her face into the woman's neck, clench her arms around the woman's waist. The two of them maneuver out to the Chevy, jerky but together, like dancing circus bears. The girl doesn't look up, so he puts his car in gear and heads out.

He threads his way through a few streets. That girl has the same problems she had two minutes ago, make no mistake about that. One hug isn't going to fix whatever's wrong. Still. Someone cared enough to come after her. He's thinking about Mark accusing him of being afraid. All along, he thought leaving was the coward's way out. He sees now, you can run away even if you stay in one place.

He's staring at himself, down a long corridor with shut doors, and none of them have doorknobs. He sees how it will be. He'll pack away the lamp that belonged to Mary and Dave's mother because it reminds him, of what? That they know what they must have always known? That he isn't worthy of their friendship? Dave will die, and he'll be too proud to attend the funeral, too afraid that Mary will see him and reproach him for his absence. Not long after, Mary will be gone, too. He'll walk by their house and wonder, did she mean to be his friend? Did she tell him that story to say, I see you and I don't care. Or did she tell him, as he had thought at the time, as a warning. What was she saying, come close or stay away? For him, it has always been stay away, until by now, he walks himself away and shuts the gate after.

He's sitting in his car, idling at a stop sign, thinking about a strange girl who turned her head into the soft neck of someone and cried. He could, he is thinking, show up on Mary's doorstep with her mother's lamp. He could hold it out to her, an offering. He has no idea what she would do or say, that's a risk. But he could do this one thing. He could give it back to her. Restored.

JUDGMENT DAY

Esther Paxton can't stand to see Leland sitting there in his overalls, his hands worrying the crocheted doilies on the recliner's armrests. It's Tuesday, and Leland sat there all day yesterday. Sunday, and Saturday, too, and the week before that. Leland's sat in that chair all the way back to June 13, when the *Reach Gazette* printed the story. The phone has stopped ringing, or else Leland leaves it off the hook. She doesn't care. Who is there to talk to anyway, unless Rosalee calls, but she won't, because Larry's still threatening to sue.

Esther's a strong-looking woman, a no-nonsense face and body to go with it, glasses and sturdy hands. Her lips clamp down tight. She wears low-heeled shoes, no jewelry, no makeup. Can't be bothered with it. She's let her hair go gray. When she taught the Bible class at the First Baptist Church, people admired her, but they didn't speak up much, and that has been the story of her life. She's outside of things, and she doesn't know why.

She opens a box of Raisin Bran and gets milk from the refrigerator. Her mouth feels dry and she craves orange juice, but she'd have to go to the store. Everybody's heard by now. The story is all over the panhandle, their bankruptcy, unpaid farmers, rumors of embezzlement. The thing is to stay strong until they can hold their heads up again. Leland sits there, not even trying. She can't forgive him for this final betrayal, never mind everything else that's come. She has no patience with that kind of indulgence, languishing in a leather recliner in the spacious den they built three years ago, not even opening the blinds, breathing in the foul air he breathed out yesterday, expecting her to rally and bring him food. She's in this too, in case he can't remember, but he's always been like that. He's taken a lot of fuss, coddling, wants his meat loaf without onions, the collars of his shirts starched. She didn't mind when the little extras made him notice her, but now he's oblivious to everything. She's hidden his gun.

She's tired of calling him to the table. She's given up on that. Oh, it's amazing the things you can adjust to, like chipping ice to wash up mornings or eating nothing but eggs through a winter. Or Leland not touching her for years. She missed that at first, an awful fire claiming her sometimes, leaving her spun out, ragged and desperate, but slowly that faded, too. She still visits a tiny grave in the Oregon Trail Cemetery. Grief pinned her to the ground once, but that was a long time ago, and she got used to the emptiness. She could eat bugs or roasted mice if she had to.

She sets the tray on the coffee table, two cereal bowls, two cups of coffee, cream and sugar for him, black for her. She can't guess what's in his head. He's never been what you'd call a deep thinker, not like her. She can remember painting rooms with him when they were young, her head off and running against the monotony of dip-brush-dip, but he reported nothing. Blank slate. She can't imagine that trick.

She forces herself to eat in the den with him. It's enough to make her puke, the way the air is stale and the darkness and his silence. "C'mon, Hon," she says, and she puts the bowl in his hands, and like a robot, he eats. So far, so good. He won't starve, and the judges won't come and carry her away for neglect or whatever they call it when a wife refuses to feed her voluntarily comatose husband.

He doesn't bother with the TV anymore. She's stopped trying to talk to him. The paper comes and she throws it out, but not before her eyes scan the headlines. Yesterday she saw that Ron Blake and Todd Birkham have declared bankruptcy. All those farmers getting foreclosed on, it's like finding another rotten plank in the flooring. Nobody will believe them if they say that's exactly what they tried to prevent. They only doctored the books to buy time. In the grain elevator business, things are never that exact. There's always borrowing from one column to another. It's just numbers, a few jagged lines on paper.

She looks at Leland sitting there, empty bowl in his hand, his mouth gone slack, and worries how he'll get through the preliminary hearing. She can't imagine how he'll pull it together to talk to a judge. She's disgusted with him, look at the drool on his shirt, his thin hair greasy, plastered to his scalp. Most nights, he sleeps in the chair. She's worried about him, but she thinks he could snap out of it. Where's his famous sense of humor? After forty-three years, she's surprised to find that she doesn't know him. He does this to her, makes her hate him while she feels sorry for him. Mostly, she doesn't know what to do.

She tugs at the bowl in his hand. He hangs on, odd, he still has that strength. Is he trying to tell her something? Sad eyes, she's seen enough of that. She plucks the bowl from his fingers and sets it on the tray. He hasn't touched his coffee, hasn't for days, but she brings it anyway, pours two cups as part of the daily ritual.

She's known Ron Blake and Todd Birkham all their lives. Once, they were snot-nosed kids in Sunday School. Todd was in Rosalee's class at the high school, puffing his cheeks out playing tuba while Rosalee threw a baton. Their wives are probably frantic. And they have children, too. Todd's oldest must be looking at college. She pictures Todd's family sitting around a kitchen table, nothing on it but a bowl of boiled eggs, fingers drumming on the Formica top. She lingers over the picture too long and hears Todd saying

it's her fault, hers and Leland's. We raised a good crop, goddam-
nit, Todd says, and his boy, the one who might have to postpone
his education, slaps the tabletop with open hands, and the eggs
bounce out of the bowl, raw eggs now, splatting on the floor, and
among broken eggshells and slimy yolks, the wife starts to cry.

Esther stands abruptly. "Guess I'll clean up, then, and go upstairs and do some sewing," she tells Leland, like she does every
day. He knows she's working on that quilt for Natalie, who will
graduate from high school next spring. She might have to mail
it. Larry says they're never going to see their grandchildren again.

"Leland," she says. She doesn't know if he hears her. He doesn't
raise his head or blink an eye.

She walks out on him, why she thinks in those terms, she
doesn't know. Good God, nobody could require her to sit there,
too, nobody expects a wife to go that far, share the same miserable mudhole as if they were two pigs. She rinses the dishes at
the kitchen sink, piles them on the drainer, wipes her hands,
and goes upstairs to a small world where she has choices, fabric
swatches of purples and greens, a variation on Drunkard's Path
that she designed herself, and when she sits to her needle and
thread, she fills her mind by humming old hymns, "Standing on
the Promises" and "Sweet Hour of Prayer," and she sticks with
it until time for lunch.

She's in the kitchen making tuna sandwiches without lettuce. She
can't remember the last time they had something fresh from the
store, but people can live on canned and frozen goods. She hears
stirring in the den and takes it for a good sign. He's up and about,
although the door is closed. Maybe he's decided to stop feeling sorry
for himself. She shouldn't have given up on him so soon. People
respond to things differently, like Reverend Fowler coming round,
pretending concern when all he wanted to know was whether they'd
have to stop their tithe. You can't predict what people will do.

Through the window above her sink, Esther spots Janet Nichols picking beans in her garden. She's a lucky woman, that Janet, a widow. Besides, everybody likes her. She has friends all over town, and the Baptist Church practically revolves around her, why not, she's perky and friendly the way Esther would like to be but isn't, no ma'am. Esther wills Janet to look up at her window. She's planned this, how one day Janet will look up, and Esther will wave at her. She's lived across the alley from Janet for fourteen years, and they've never neighbored except over the fence or when they ran into each other at the Jack & Jill. It will have to be a different kind of wave, a signal, not a plea for pity. Esther doesn't want that. It will be a little flick of the wrist wave, an almost beckoning, a come hither, a "drop whatever you're doing and rescue me" kind of wave, but she doesn't want to look over-anxious, either. In the mirror, when she's practiced, the wave looks right to her, different than a casual greeting but not frantic.

Esther focuses all her attention on Janet, but Janet doesn't look up at the window. She's intent on picking beans, stupid cow, unaware of anything around her but herself. If she were any kind of neighbor, she'd know they're having a hard time over here. A good neighbor would know how to care without intruding, the way Esther had done when Janet's husband died. She sent a card, kept a discreet distance, watched for opportunities, picked up a dropped shirt from Janet's clothesline, deadheaded the irises that bordered the alley. She doesn't like to poke her nose in other people's business, hovering the way some women do. Instead, Esther left hints: I'm here if you need me. That's all she wants now, some sign beyond the hasty message scrawled in the margins of their newspaper— "Traitors"—or the dead robin someone laid out on their front stoop, its wings stiff and splayed open, nothing a cat could have done.

Esther loads up her lunch tray, two tuna sandwiches on plates, mayo, no lettuce, a pile of potato chips for each, glasses of iced tea. She opens the door to the den, glances toward the chair, is pleased to see that Leland, for once, is not sitting in it. Her eyes adjust to the dim light. He's up, but what the hell's he doing? He's tearing pages from books and gluing them to the paneling. He's got a jar of rubber cement—thank God for that, easy to remove—he's gluing like mad, and when she stops him and yanks on his arm, he turns glassy eyes on her.

"Paper. Paper. The rays can't get through the paper. See, Esther? See?" His fingers jiggle. His voice rasps.

"What rays, Leland?" She tries to keep her voice calm, like she used to do on the farm when approaching a skittish horse.

"They have microphones everywhere." He's whispering now, shielding his mouth with his open hand. "I thought I could hide in this room, but the microphones. They send out rays that bounce off everything. Not paper, though, see?"

Her hand reaches out to him, her fingers fluttering aimlessly in the air between them. Several Lelands dance before her and retreat, the boy who waltzed her around the Veterans' Hall, the frightened young man who sobbed when their baby died, the fiddle-playing jokester, all the Lelands she has known and loved turn their backs on her, and she is left with this stranger. She withdraws her hand. "Who's sending the rays?" she asks, but he's too far gone. Could be the sheriff, could be the Deacon Board, makes no difference, and she can hardly get him to sit still long enough to eat his sandwich.

She assesses the situation. He's crazy, but he's moving. He's up and taking control over what little of his life he can, and she guesses that's better than the way he was before. Maybe after he papers the whole room, he'll settle down and get some peace. Maybe this is a primitive form of therapy, like screaming into a pillow, which she has tried on several occasions. Maybe his motion will keep him going right out the door and fishing. He's all talk now, his voice rising with excitement, but what he says is gibberish, crazy stuff about rays and spies and how Larry's out to kill him.

She gathers up four more jars of rubber cement that she finds around the house. She rescues a few books she can't bear to have torn apart, *Jane Eyre* and *Robinson Crusoe* and what's left of the family Bible. He's already torn out the Book of Revelation, the fiery phrases beaming off the pine paneling, "Babylon and smoke," "hail and fire," "woe, woe, woe to those who dwell on the earth." She shuts her mind against the damnation from the Lord and goes upstairs to her scissors, her thread, her perfectly cut squares and rectangles. Hell on earth, that's what she thinks. Who needs to wait for eternity? She whacks herself good on the side of the face to keep from crying, and she gets down to work.

She peeks in at him before she starts their supper. The den is a good-sized room and he's got one whole wall done, top to bottom, pages fluttering in the air conditioning, upside down, sideways. He's not paying the least attention to what's on the paper. It could be typing paper as far as he's concerned, but it takes him longer to tear pages from the books, and she thinks the longer this takes the better, because he's occupied.

It's still light out. Summer sun takes a long time to go down, and the days seem endless. Rosalee could call, if she had half a mind to. Too bad they live so far away, down there in Grand Island. She's sure Rosalee would pop over if she lived here, in spite of Larry. Maybe to spite Larry, although Esther's never picked up on any animosity between Rosalee and Larry. In fact, Rosalee seems to think Larry's the be-all and end-all, but then, you never know what's in a marriage, take Esther's for example, who would have guessed that she and Leland were engaged in a life of crime? Leland never should have asked Larry to get him off or speak to the judge. She could have told Leland that, if he'd bothered to check with her first, Larry being such a self-righteous little prick, acting like he's the only person in recent history to pass the bar exam. "I could be disbarred," he'd whined, as if Leland had asked him to store heroin or hide a dismembered body. Rosalee could call.

Esther gets busy frying the hamburger she's thawed from the freezer. She cooks up only half a pound because her supply is getting low, and why should she be the one to subject herself to public scrutiny? As long as Hal keeps delivering milk and eggs to the door, they can last a long time on what she's got put by in the pantry and the freezer. She takes a box of Hamburger Helper off the shelf. She despises this stuff, but it makes the meat stretch farther. She keeps it on hand for church potlucks.

She finds a shriveled cucumber in the refrigerator, ah, a green vegetable, washes it off under the tap. She looks across the alley at Janet's, but everything is quiet. Esther's neighbor, that Michael somebody who married the Swartz girl, is throwing more junk on an already overflowing pile in the alley. He's practically ruined that place, nothing but dirt in the yard, old tires and pieces of two-by-four piled out back, big fat slob of a man, his bare chest matted with hair, belly hanging over his pants top. He's yelling at somebody cowering by the garage. He's swearing, striking his closed fist in an open palm. Esther stretches to turn the water off when she sees Michael reach out and grab whoever's standing in the shadows. He yanks his son by the hair, the boy can't be much more than ten or eleven, what's his name, his name, and while Esther rummages through her mind for the child's name, her eyes register the blows to his face, closed-fisted, his father pummeling the boy like he's a punching bag. Shocked, she stands too long. The boy throws his arms up to protect his head. The father is kicking him now, kicking him while the child curls up in the dirt.

Esther's hand fumbles for the telephone, she has the receiver off the hook, her finger in the dial, she's looking for the sheriff's number, but how can she call? How can she report her neighbor when the whole town has branded them? Who will believe her? Even if they do, everybody knows these domestic abuse cases are a lost cause, and that's the Swartz girl who's lived here all her life. The gossip will kill her, she'll be papering her living room with pages of books. There would be questions. The sheriff, maybe Pastor Fowler, the Deacons, all the self-appointed judges swarming through their house, looking at Leland and what he's come to. Esther's hand trembles.

She may have misjudged the whole thing. She's been under a lot of stress. Parents need to discipline their children. Sometimes it gets out of hand, but children recover. Her father smacked her sometimes, her brothers more often, but she grew up. She turns her head, sees the boy lying in the dirt, his father walking away. It's over, then. The damage done. There's nothing left for her to do. She can't right all the wrongs in this world.

She breathes easier, still watching when the father turns. He's back on the boy, straddling him, banging his head into the ground. The boy's hands flail wildly, helpless against his father's brute strength. She's the only witness, her view a narrow tunnel created by the sides of both houses and their shed. The boy's name is Samuel. She drops the phone on the cradle. By the time she reaches the sheriff or 911, Samuel could be dead. Brain damaged. Her eyes fixed out the window, she gropes through the flour canister and pulls out Leland's gun. She dumps the sugar bowl to find the bullets. She knows how to load the thing, Leland made her learn to fire it when she worked late in the office at the elevator. She knows how to aim and shoot straight through the heart of a target. She prays Janet is home to call the cops and has enough guts to do it. Samuel, Samuel, she mutters, his name an incantation on her tongue. Leland's in his never-never land, pasting paper on walls to ward off unseen enemies, while she stands with a cocked gun in their kitchen. She barks out a short laugh. She's thinking that she hopes Rosalee won't have to know, as she opens the back door, steps outside in the full glare of the sun, aims the pistol at the bleached blue sky, and fires.

ALL THE WILDNESS IN HER

Janet never should have accepted that gift from Leland. He wanted to thank her for all she'd done for Esther. That poor woman, shrinking from cancer. Esther died a year ago, and Janet has hardly seen or spoken to Leland since. When he phoned, Janet tried to tell him he'd no need to give her anything. He insisted. He said Rosalee thought it would be all right. Janet knows he's lonely, and since Rosalee approved, what's the harm? She agreed to meet him in the alley between their houses. She doesn't want him coming to the door.

Broad daylight, he hands her a flat, narrow box. She doesn't open it. Looking past his shoulder, she sees nothing but gravel and spent hollyhocks against her neighbor's garage. The air smells like fall, of wet decay, yet crisp. She slides the box down, close to her hip, hiding it inside her palm and wrist.

She's shocked at the look of him, the white hair, sagging skin. Her own short hair is gray, full and wavy. She looks a bit like a schoolmarm, buttoned up, proper, a crisp cotton blouse worn loose over beige pants. She stays fit, mows her own grass, scoops her walks, bends over rows of greens and burgeoning tomato plants in her garden. She takes a few medications, heart, mostly. Her body has compressed. She's shorter, heavy breasts sagging toward what passes for a waistline. She hates the droop of her jaw, the loss of definition between face and neck, but you can't fight gravity. She's not one to carry on about it. Freckled as a girl, her face, arms, and hands are mottled with brown age spots. Even so, she's alarmed by the change in Leland. He must be, what, eighty-five? A few years younger than her.

"How are you, Leland?"

He shrugs. "You know."

She does know. She's been widowed. Long time ago, but it sticks with you. She's lived across this alley from Leland and Esther for over thirty years, but she didn't know them beyond a passing acquaintance until Esther took sick. Of course, she knew about that rough time they had. The bankruptcy. They stuck it out, though. Once the target of gossip, they had become legends of a certain kind.

"Well, it's hard." At a loss for what else to say, she nods and turns back to her house. She knows he'd like to talk. He's a talker. She's scared someone will see them, make this out to be something it isn't, though why anybody should care what two old coots do on an autumn day is beyond her reckoning. She doesn't stop to consider why she cares what people think. Conditioned by a lifetime of small town living, she draws her curtains at night. Puts her trash in sealed bags.

She perches on the edge of her bed, the lavender chenille worn smooth from years of sitting in this exact spot to put on her shoes or talk on the bedside phone. She lifts the lid off the box. A bracelet winks up at her, gold discs with small stones, all different colors. Must be glass, though it looks expensive. Damn fool. He ought to know she can't manage the clasp. Let him to try to put a bracelet on himself at this age.

She holds it up to the light. Her eyes aren't what they used to be. The jewels twinkle, green, yellow, pink. It's a pretty thing, she does admit that.

She ought to thank him proper. She sits at her kitchen table to write a note but can't shape the words. She pictures the mailman, that Jerry, the smirk on his face. Plus, a note could lie around, if Leland wasn't careful, and she's never known Leland to be careful. Shocking, really. When Esther took sick, Leland was helpless. Couldn't even boil soup. Some men are like that, but not her Carl. Carl liked cooking more than she did, was better at it. Ribs, his specialty, dry rub. She smacks her lips.

Not thinking more about it, she calls Leland's house, the number still in her memory from those times with Esther.

When he answers, Leland's voice sounds gruff. Not like him, in real life.

"I called to thank you," she says.

"Did you like it?" There, that high whine at the end. That's more like him.

"It's beautiful." She doesn't say, I can't wear it, you damn fool.

"Rosalee helped pick it out."

"Oh." She should have known. She sinks a little, a surprise to herself.

"It was my idea."

Okay, then. Feeling bold, she says, "Some time, if you want to drive out to the farm, I wouldn't mind."

The three of them drove out to that farm often, Esther in the backseat with blankets and pillows. They watched the sunsets, the pheasants floating above the wild hay. Janet has missed that bit of country. It took her back to her childhood.

Months go by, robins show up, the forsythia blooms, and one day Leland calls. "Thought I'd take you up on that offer," he says.

She's not coy. Sees no point. "I'd like that," she says.

"What about now?"

She has a day planned, but it can wait. There's little urgency left in her goings-on. "I'll meet you in the alley."

They drive the ten minutes to the farm. If there's a coal train, it can take fifteen or twenty, but the tracks are empty today. Her heart speeds up when Leland pulls into the long drive. There's that meadow, crowning with larkspur. Across the creek. Past the windmill and into the yard. The house isn't much, never has been. Marty waves from the front porch. Having Marty on the place is one step shy of it being vacant. Leland keeps him around to ward off thieves. That, and for old time's sake.

Leland drives out past the alfalfa field, along the old windbreak creaking with age. He stops the car in that north pasture. Leland doesn't run livestock anymore, so this stretch has reverted to prairie. It's her favorite part of the place, wild and bountiful, flooded with insects and birdsong, monarch butterflies scavenging for milkweed, dragonflies with cellophane wings, dark-veined like stained-glass windows. Leland still keeps bees in this section, stacked hives abuzz. The honey is pure amber, dark and golden. He pays somebody to harvest the honey now, having lost the dexterity to move fluidly and not excite the hive. They stop under a stand of cottonwoods. She breathes in the scent of sweet clover and sighs.

"Beautiful," she says.

"I remember how you liked it," Leland says.

They sit for a while, not talking much. Old companions with shared history. Janet soaks in the ease of it, the pleasantness. She wants nothing more than this, friendship and a whiff of countryside.

He doesn't call for a while, and then one day he does. She's eager for it, and that bothers her. He says he's got a surprise for her. Something lights up in her, and that bothers her, too. She doesn't want to count on anything from this man. He's not steady. Plus, she's too old to start up any fuss.

She agrees to meet him in the alley, settles into his car, rides with him out to the farm. He looks boyish, smiling like he's got a big secret. She's annoyed, with him and with herself. Such damn fools, the both of them. What's he got to show her? A new litter of barnyard kittens? A prairie plant they've not noticed before? How big the alfalfa has gotten?

She's trying to decide whether she'll give him the satisfaction of thinking he's pleased her, the way a person fakes a response to an unwanted surprise party, one your best friend doesn't even attend and you'd rather be free to take your Saturday night bath, when he pulls up alongside the barn and stops the car. There's some newfangled contraption parked there that looks like an overgrown tricycle.

Leland scrambles out, giddy as hot grease on a griddle. "C'mon," he says. With some difficulty, he works a stiff leg over and straddles the seat. Janet has gotten herself out of the car, but she hasn't strayed far from the front fender. "Git on," Leland says.

He grins at her, and she sees a flash of the man he once must have been. She suppresses a giggle, throws a leg over the seat, and snuggles behind him. He flips a switch that sputters the engine to life. "Hang on," he yells. The machine lurches forward. She almost topples off the back, but she grabs at his waist in time. Away they go, following rutted trails, over the jangling cattle gate, alongside the cloying alfalfa, back to the big irrigation ditch, and the whole time she clings to Leland, his body pressed against her heavy breasts, dust clouding her face, thinking she should have worn more sunscreen. Sheer madness, the two of them out there like that, but oh, it's fun. She laughs out loud, lays her head back, and closes her eyes, the way a girl does who's swinging high, high, surrendering to the open sky and all the wildness in her.

After that, they go riding three or four times a week. He calls first. She meets him in the alley. Their favorite time of day is dusk.

Sometimes they stop and pick up hamburgers at Hardee's. They stick the hamburgers and a thermos of coffee in the sidecar, climb on the three-wheeler, and ride across Leland's land. They stroll through the twilight, past the cattails and the marsh grass, among the nodding goldenrod. They laugh and talk, voices bobbing up and down under the blossoming sky. He drops her in the alley back in town. Nobody knows.

One day, mid July, the cicadas buzz up a symphony. Heat wobbles in the thick air. Humidity slathers their skin. They pick raspberries, lips and fingers stained red. Juice dribbles down Leland's chin, and with a quavering thumb, Janet wipes it off. A creek wraps through Leland's land, and they ride the three-wheeler to the backstretch, hidden from house or road.

"Janet," Leland says, still astride the seat. She can't read his face, but she hears the lightness in his voice. "Have you ever gone wading in a creek?"

Janet chuckles. "Oh, sure, Leland. Lots of times."

Careful to avoid the thorny wild roses, keeping an eye out for poison ivy, they thread their way to the creek bank and lower themselves in the shade of a Russian olive tree. Laughing, they peel off their shoes and socks. She tries not to notice his yellow, ridged toenails. Hopes he doesn't zero in on the blue veins gorged above her ankles. They each roll up their pant legs. Leland gets first to his hands and knees, then pulls himself to his feet and holds a hand out to her. Worried that the creek bed might be slippery, they cling to each other and step gingerly into the water. It has occurred to her that if he fell or had a heart attack or a stroke, she'd have no way to get help. She doesn't know how to drive that thing. With her eyesight, she couldn't find her way back to the house. Eventually Marty would come looking for them, but by then, one or the other could be in a world of hurt. Or dead.

They feel their way along the creek bed, wincing at sharp rocks, teetering toward one another for balance. The cool water bathes her parched skin. The sandy creek bottom welcomes her poor old feet, as if to say, where have you been all these years?

They walk straight out into the middle and a few yards along with the creek's flow, when Leland stops. She stops, too, rather than risk falling over.

"Janet, have you ever been kissed in a creek?"

He tosses this remark over his shoulder, his eyes focused on the bank farthest away from her, so if she laughs him off or disapproves, he can pretend he was joking. She sees through his game.

"No, Leland." Her voice emerges soft and breathy, no wind left in her. "I don't believe I have."

When he turns to face her, she's ready for him. His lips are surprisingly soft. She's not sure what she expected. An old man's mouth. Dry and chapped. He knows what a good kiss is made of, tender and lingering, and the warmth that spreads through her body, even down there, surprises her. She reaches for him with the hand he's not holding, maybe (she thinks later) for balance, but he wraps his arm around her, too, and they kiss again.

Sweet, that's all she's thinking, there among the meadowlarks and cattails, her toes digging for traction in the sandy creek bed.

There's quite a lot of kissing after that. When she gets in the car in the alley, she scoots over close to him. Sometimes she rests her hand on his thigh while he's driving. She waits for his call eagerly. They broaden their activities beyond the farm, long drives in the countryside, supper in Scottsbluff, always out of town, nothing to get the gossips wagging. She's grateful for his discretion. She wonders if she should cook him a meal, but it'd be awkward, sneaking him in and out the back door, hoping nobody sees. She keeps up her activities, the card group on Sunday afternoons, Bible study on Tuesdays, shocked to realize how much open time there must have been in her life before. She doesn't worry about

Esther, who's dead and not coming back and would never begrudge the living a moment of happiness. No, it's not Esther that prompts them to this secrecy. Their—what is it exactly, not affair (good heavens), nor relationship—well, special friendship, feels somehow sacred. A private space they've created, like children who carve a haven out of hay bales, away from prying eyes of the adult and disapproving world. Janet tells only her sister that she's been riding with a man on a three-wheeler.

Her sister, who lives far away in Ohio and has been married fifty-seven years, asks, "Where's this going?"

"We're friends." Janet clamps her lips to keep the lilt out of her voice.

"Are you sure that's all?"

"Oh, yes," Janet says, that breathless feeling coming over her again.

She does entertain—thoughts. No, she doesn't want to get married again. They're too old. One or the other of them will take sick. Or die. She doesn't want to go through being widowed again. She doesn't want that kind of pain. She doesn't want to put another man to bed, like she did Carl, who died a long slow death from a combination of emphysema and corrosive arteries.

Plus, she's used to living alone. She and Carl found each other too late for children. He was a bachelor farmer, and she a spinster schoolteacher from down by Ogallala. They met at a dance at the Legion, and he stepped all over her feet. His embarrassment won her heart, long before he spoke of any affection for her. They'd made a good life together, though they only had ten years before he took sick. They moved to town, then. Sold the farm to his distant cousins. She nursed him until he died. Too young for Social Security, she went back to teaching history until she could retire. With her pension, Social Security, and proceeds from the farm sale, she's doing all right.

Without Carl or anyone else to answer to, she's made the house her own. The year after Carl died, she painted the kitchen ceiling red. She gets some looks from the women in the Bible study, but she's never tired of that ceiling. It speaks to her of possibility. When she got interested in Civil War history, she hung a corkboard on the dining room wall and charted the battlefields, marking each site with different colored flags according to who won; blue for Union, red for Confederate. She loves opera, unheard of among her friends out here on the prairie, and she cranks up the volume on her old (but plenty good) record player, the walls humming plaintive song. She doubts very much if Leland would tolerate a red ceiling, and she knows for a fact he has no appreciation for opera.

But, where is this going? If he asks, she would have to consider marriage, wouldn't she? Otherwise, what is she doing? She'd forgotten how lovely and invigorating the feeling that you matter to someone in a special way. She does care for him. It's too late to pretend otherwise, and she's not going to lie to herself about it. Growing old might be less fearsome together.

She holds forth in this way, arguing with herself, refuting, rebutting, preparing, because any fool can see that they can't simply go on riding into the sunset and kissing under the cottonwoods and parting in the back alley. Although, that is precisely what she wants. To simply go on, uncomplicated, like any young thing too naïve to consider the consequences of love.

One day Leland parks the three-wheeler under the stand of cottonwoods. It's late afternoon, the time of long shadows when the sun drops toward the edge of the world. He spreads a blanket, tan and red striped. She holds her hand off the edge of the blanket, letting a clump of prairie grass tickle her palm.

"Can I ask you something, Janet?"

She nods. Here it comes, she thinks. She perks up, interested to see what answer she will give.

"What do you think about sex?" he says.

Well, that is a surprise. Janet almost laughs. "What do you mean?"

"Sex. Do you like it?"

"What kind of question is that?" She's thinking there are some things you do, and you don't have to talk about them.

"You like kissing, don't you?"

"Well, Leland." She pulls herself up, sits as tall as she can, wraps her arms around her bent knees. She prides herself on her flexibility. Not many women her age can sit like this. "I'm not dead."

"That's just it. We may not have that much time. I like you. When two people enjoy each other, they want to be close."

"I think sex is a beautiful thing."

"I'm glad you said that."

"Between two married people." She says this plain. She's thinking this is an odd conversation for a courtship. At their age.

"Nobody said anything about marriage."

"Oh." Oh dear. Oh my. She hadn't considered . . . How could he think that? How could he even imagine she'd . . . ? She looks away, embarrassed.

"Well, come on, now. We're too old to complicate our lives like that."

He's put on his coaxing voice, the one he uses to nicker to the horses across the fence, get them to come for the apples in his hand. If he thinks she'll come running across the pasture to eat out of his hand, he has another think coming.

She rises to her feet with as much dignity as she can muster. "Take me home, Leland."

It's ruined after that. Sex is all he can talk about. Every outing ends, sooner or later, with him trying to talk her into doing something she simply cannot, will not do.

"People will talk," she says.

"Who cares?"

"I do. I have to live in this town."

"We can go out of town."

"I'm not going to sneak around."

"You could just leave your back door unlocked," he tries. "I could slip in and out, be gone by morning."

She doesn't dignify this with an answer.

"I don't believe in sex outside of marriage," she says.

"C'mon, Janet. Where've you been? This is the modern world."

"I don't care what others do. That's their choice."

"What are you afraid of? You're not going to get pregnant."

How dare he make her feel like an old relic? She looks him straight in the eye, defiant. "I don't believe in it."

"God gave us these desires. Why wouldn't he want us to enjoy them?"

"Don't blame God for this."

"I'm not blaming anybody."

"You're saying it's God's fault. You're using God to justify your own desires."

"So are you." His voice rises higher. It's not a pleasant sound.

"I'm talking about my faith. Not desires."

"You don't have any desires."

"That's not fair."

"I don't think you do. I don't think you feel anything."

She says nothing. How can she say anything to this man?

"Now you're mad."

"I'm not mad."

"You sure look mad."

"I'm disappointed."

"Esther never wanted sex," he tells her one day.

She knows that's a lie. She wonders if he has had affairs, all along. Justified them with his crazy talk of God-given desire.

She starts to resent how he doesn't want to be seen with her. They attend the same church, but they never sit together. He greets her the same way he greets all the other widows, a curt nod as he passes by. Plus, he's always talking about his investments. Why tell her he's rich when he has no intention of sharing his wealth with her? And why, if he's so loaded, didn't he feel any obligation to pay back those farmers? He doesn't want to risk dying first and have it all go to her instead of Rosalee. She knows what a prenuptial agreement is, but he's beyond even that. He doesn't want to share his home, his life. He wants a little back door hanky-panky, that's all. She feels used. And dirty.

Her sister is of no help.

"You said you didn't want to marry him."

"I don't."

"But you seem angry that he doesn't ask you to marry him?"

"You'd be mad, too, if somebody you thought cared about you expected sex but no commitment."

"Oh, I don't know."

"C'mon."

"It's the times. My own grandchildren . . ."

"That's different."

"If he asked, would you say no?"

"I guess we'll never find out." With that, Janet hangs up.

Not long after this conversation, Leland picks her up and tells her to scoot over by the door. "Don't sit by me, if you don't mean it."

"All right." She hugs the door, head turned away, her mind out the window and riding hard over turbulent waves.

He doesn't take her to the farm. Instead, they drive out south of town to Courthouse and Jail Rocks, deserted sandstone monuments haunting the prairie. Legend has it that Indians used to keep prisoners here.

He stops the car, turns to look at her. "I thought I could wear you down," he says.

Tight-lipped, she says, "Then you don't know me very well."

"No. I guess I don't."

She has nothing to say to that. They don't look at each other.

"Hell," he says. "I don't even know if I can do it. Maybe I got too old."

She has to laugh at that. He laughs, too. Then, it seems all right between them. They sit there a while, not bothering to get out of the car, enjoying the sagebrush and yuccas, the lone eagle soaring overhead, the grasshoppers springing from ragweed. He takes her home and drops her in the alley. They each smile, though he does not reach for her to kiss her. She gets out of the car and knows he will not call again.

Months go by, another Thanksgiving, then Christmas, Valentine's Day. After Easter, she plants another garden, picks early radishes and lettuce. When her sister asks, "What ever happened to Leland?" she answers, "We're friends."

One day while shopping in the drug store for Q-tips and toothpaste, she hears that Leland has had a stroke. He's lost the use of one side of his body, though they say his mind is good.

Janet frets over him, but she can't drive. She hears he's in a nursing home in Scottsbluff. One Sunday, her pastor stops her briefly after the Sunday service. Pastor Glen is a young man; people like him. He's got a houseful of kids, and that's always a good sign.

"Janet," Pastor says. "I'm driving up to see Leland on Tuesday. I wondered if you'd care to ride along."

She peers into the pastor's face, sees only kindness. She should have known nothing is a secret in this town.

"I'd like that," she says.

At the nursing home, the pastor visits for a few minutes, offers a prayer over Leland's ruined body, then finds an excuse to leave the room. Janet pulls a chair next to Leland's bed, puts her hand over his good hand. His other hand lies inert against his side. He has no use of one side of his body, but he's propped up against the headboard.

"Janet. I'm glad to see you."

He looks as though he might cry. Janet pats his hand. "Now, now Leland. I'm here."

She looks around his room. Small, the way they are. Odors, something between disinfectant and musty, old body smell. On a set of built-in shelves, she sees he has a picture of the farm, Rosalee and her family.

"Remember when we picked raspberries?" he says.

"Of course, Leland."

"And feeding the horses over the fence."

She nods, though shame creeps through her, remembering how she thought of Leland coaxing her like those horses. Her throat feels full, and she's afraid if she tries to speak, she'll embarrass both of them.

"And the creek." He waggles his eyebrows a bit. She's relieved to see his rakish humor intact.

She rises and leans over to kiss his weathered and whiskery cheek. Low and in his ear, she says, "We had a wonderful summer."

He grabs at her arm, his grasp surprisingly strong. His jaw trembles. "Janet, I don't want to live like this."

"Shhh." She pats him on the back.

"I want to go home."

"I know you do."

"They won't let me out of here."

She struggles to quiet him, pats his back, but he grows only more distressed. She sits on the edge of the bed, puts her arm around his shoulders, tries to draw his head to her breast. He's stiff and heavy, so she swings her legs up on the bed, and soon she's lying with him, cradling him as best she can. He quiets, except for the tears soaking into her blouse front. "Now, now," she says, and he's calm as long as she doesn't try to move away from him, which she has no intention of doing. She's thinking it's too bad that he didn't die when he had the chance. He's trapped now. He knows it, and she knows it, too.

Eventually, the pastor will come to collect her for the ride home or a nurse will want to take Leland to physical therapy, and they'll find her in this undignified pose, lying like a schoolgirl on the edge of a man's bed, her clothes twisted awry from the awkwardness of it. She will have to stand in front of them and say good-bye. Likely, she'll note pity and condescension in their eyes, that special combo reserved for the very old, but what does any of that matter now? Might as well stop the clocks, turn off the telephones. What's done is done, and she braces herself for all that may be required of her.

Waiting for the pastor, she strokes Leland's cheek. "Oh, my dear," she says. "My poor dear."

FIRE ON HIS MIND

Afterward, Tom bought smoke alarms and put them in every room of the house. He staged fire drills day and night, especially night, when he stood with a stopwatch and timed Helen and his boys, Alex and Trent, while they tumbled out of beds and groped their way to the yard. Once he bolted the door from the outside to see if they would figure out what to do. When they didn't emerge from the house, he was furious.

"What the hell are you thinking?" he stormed. They were gathered in the living room. Helen, eyes heavy with sleep, slumped on the tattered couch in a thin yellow tank top and drawstring cotton shorts. She'd thrown on a flowered robe to hide her nipples from the boys. That action alone cost precious seconds. He tipped the reading lamp to shine in their faces. Helen squinted and lifted a hand, but the boys, seven and nine, looked at him wide-eyed. Scared, and well they should be. They could have burned to death.

"Dad, what did you want us to do?" Alex asked.

"Break a window." He heard himself shouting. "Pick up any goddamn chair and throw it through the glass."

"But Dad, when I broke a window throwing a football, you got mad," Trent said.

He shook his head, unable to believe they could not comprehend the seriousness of this. His wife, too. Nodding away there.

"When there's fire . . . ," he began.

"But it wasn't a fire," Alex said. "It was you blowing your whistle. Like last time."

He knelt in front of them. He took each of his boys by the arm. Sitting there in their skivvies with knobby knees and scrawny chests, they looked like baby birds. "When you hear this whistle, I want you to see fire. I want you to smell fire. And then, you do whatever it takes to get the hell out of this house. Now, am I clear?"

The boys glanced at each other. He knew that look. In another five, six years they'd be looking at each other like that all the time, as if their old man was loco. Let them.

The first week he took a lot of showers. Washed himself over and over and still could not get the stench out of his hair. When he'd finally found those two teenagers huddled together behind a closet door, their skin had been black and crispy. He didn't tell Helen that. He'd reached out, his volunteer fireman's glove awkward and thick and protecting him, and the boy's shoulder caved like a marshmallow cooked too long over coals. That crinkled coating that slakes away.

People talked about it for days. At the lunch counter in Brenda's Café, in the vestibule of the Methodist Church, on the four corners of Main and Elm. Sweet old Mrs. Willow walked it into Tom's pharmacy.

"Too bad about that poor family, wasn't it?" she said.

He busied himself behind the counter. In his white lab coat and dark framed glasses he looked ordinary enough, his sandy hair short and neatly combed.

"Did you know them?"

Tom shook his head.

"Shirttail relation to the Slokems," Mrs. Willow said. "Only been here a couple of months."

Tom handed her the usual blood pressure medication.

"I heard the mother ran straight through the fire with the two little ones. She must've thought those older kids would follow." She blinked at him once, twice, her eyes magnetized behind thick lenses.

"Will that be all?" He stood at the old-fashioned cash register, his hand poised to ring up the sale. Normally he loved the pearl keys, the ka-ching of the tray opening. He found comfort in the swivel stools and soda fountain, the amber and liquor green medicine bottles displayed on shelves. He'd collected these relics himself from small towns throughout the panhandle. Today, however, they only reminded him that he could not recreate the past. He could no more resurrect the simpler, sweeter time he'd seen in Norman Rockwell paintings than he could bring those two teenagers or his own dead parents back to life.

"Why didn't they go out the back door?" Mrs. Willow waited for his reply.

Sweat trickled from his armpits. The air stale and full of soot. "I don't know," he said, his voice a hoarse whisper. "They probably died before the fire got to them. Smoke inhalation."

At night, with fire on his mind, he tucked his boys in bed. He hovered over them, one bunk, then the other, smoothed cowboy sheets around slim shoulders, brushed cheeks with his fingers.

"Dad?" Alex said.

"Yeah."

"You said we can't take anything with us."

Tom hesitated. He didn't want them having nightmares. Still.

"That's right." He sat on the edge of the lower bunk.

"What about Bilko?" Bilko, the fat calico cat.

"Nope. Everybody gets themselves out. That's the way it works."

"But, Dad," Trent said, from the upper bunk. "What if I fell down and broke my leg? Would you help me?"

He stood, reached out, and smoothed the wrinkles between his son's eyes with his thumb. "'Course I would. It's my job to help you. I'm a fireman." The grin on Trent's face, goofy and sweet, filled him with despair.

"Come to bed, Tom," Helen said. She leaned against the doorjamb, arms crossed. He lay sprawled on the couch in the back den, the TV muted but flickering with bad news. He hadn't been able to sleep. He got up and slathered Vicks under his nose to mask the putrid odor of smoldering flesh. He made hot milk but could not drink it. He did forty push-ups.

"They shouldn't let people live in those shacks," he said. He could see the worry in Helen's eyes, the tension around her mouth. He'd been telling her for days not to drive without her seat belt. To get the carbon monoxide levels checked in the house. To wear double gloves when she drew blood from hospital patients. On her days off, he didn't want her going down in the basement if he wasn't home. What if an electrical wire came loose, and she dangled her fingers in the laundry tub?

Helen held out her hand. He let her lead him to their room, up the stairs. He slid in bed beside her and feigned sleep. He waited until Helen's breathing deepened, then opened his eyes. Nightly now, his parents' accident invaded his dreams. He'd been away in college at the time, but lately he watches by the side of the road or floats above the car. He hears his mother scream, but he can do nothing, and then he wakes more wrung out than when he went to bed. Not my fault, not my fault, Tom muttered now, as he propped himself up with two pillows, cocked his ear to listen for intruders, and waited for dawn.

Three weeks after the fire he drove past the remains of the shack. The concrete foundation lay exposed, littered with blackened wood and debris. Particles of ash drifted through the air whenever the breeze stirred.

He stopped his car, covered his nose and mouth with a handkerchief. He rolled down the window to get a clearer view but saw no one. Not that he expected to. The mother and two younger children were long gone. The itinerant husband, too.

He noticed a car he'd not seen before parked at the neighboring shack. A maroon hatchback Focus. Nice car, for drifters. He studied the front door, the jagged tear in the screen. Through the window he caught the blue light of a television.

The front door opened and a boy stepped out, a kid about Trent's age, red hair, skinny, wearing a sweatshirt and jeans. He carried a baseball bat. The kid started swinging the bat wildly, not like he was lining up for a pitch, just flailing away at the air. He took a swipe at the car parked in the drive. Whack. Then straightened up and looked furtively toward the house. When no one came running out the door, he took another swing at the fender. Whack. Even from his seat in the car, Tom could tell he'd left a couple good dents. The kid swung and then wiped his nose. Christ. These people.

Over pancakes, he warned them. "Stay away from that new kid at school." Helen looked up from the lunches she was packing. She slathered minced ham with mayonnaise, a spawning ground for bacteria.

"He's in my class," Trent said.

"See," Tom said, not at all sure what he meant.

"What's wrong with him?" Trent said.

Tom stopped to consider, swirled sludgy coffee around his mouth to buy some time. "He could be dangerous."

"Tom!" Helen, up on her high horse again.

"Look, I know some things."

"What things?" She pointed her loaded paring knife at him.

"What's his name?" Alex asked.

"Manson," Trent said.

"You mean, that's his last name?" Tom wiped at his coffee mustache with the back of his hand.

"First. He said he was named after Charles somebody."

"Jesus H," Tom muttered. That look again from Helen.

"Jesus H," Alex echoed. Tom reached behind Trent and bopped Alex on the back of the head. At the same time he raised his eyebrows and nodded toward Helen, and Alex grinned. Tom put his hand over the sharp pain in his chest.

The call came from Margaret Seward, the principal over at the school. Later he wouldn't remember what she'd said. He heard Trent's name, the alarm in her voice, and he bolted. In the tiny parking lot behind the drug store, his car was wedged in by Dr. Feldman's monstrous Buick. Tom crashed his fist down on a rear fender, yelped in pain, and took off running. For eight blocks he carried an image of Trent bloody and gasping. All it takes is a baseball in the throat. A science experiment gone amok. They should have homeschooled the boys.

He rounded the corner, saw a police car in front of the school, and plunged into the building. Ellen met him in the foyer, her face pasty above her white uniform like a mask on a Halloween nurse. She put her hand on his chest and said, "Breathe."

He raised his arm to brush her off, but the pain doubled him in half. Her hand moved to his back. "Breathe, Tom."

"Is he dead?" he managed to croak before coughing.

"No, no. God help us. He's in the OR."

He lifted his head, and through the window into the school office he saw Trent sitting on a couch. Margaret was perched beside him, alert and wary, watching him the way you might a foreigner or a poisonous insect. Trent's head was down, but he wasn't bleeding. He wasn't even crying.

Tom lifted his finger and pointed. "He's right there."

"Not Trent. The other boy. He's in the OR."

"What other boy?" Tom said.

"Didn't they tell you what happened?"

He shook his head, still fighting for breath. "All I heard was Trent in trouble, and I took off."

Margaret stepped to the door and motioned for them to come in. She'd moved Trent into the secretary's office. Jeffrey Klotsch, wearing his police uniform, stood with arms folded, working hard to look stern and professional. Tom had gone to school with Jeffrey and knew that he'd flunked math two years in a row.

"Jeffrey," Tom said. Jeffrey nodded, but his eyes fished around the room.

"What the hell's going on here?" Tom said. "I want to see my son."

"Why don't we all sit down," Margaret said.

The women coaxed him with murmurs and tugs on his arm. Jeffrey loomed there, not budging until Tom lowered himself to the couch beside Ellen. Margaret sat across from them. Jeffrey plopped his overweight frame on a chair set at a right angle. Tom watched Jeffrey out of the corner of his eye while Margaret explained the situation.

Trent's class had gone to the river on a science expedition. On the way back, Manson walked ahead. The second graders were at recess, and Alex had bent down to pick up a leaf when his jacket caught on the fence. Manson bent over to help him, and that's when Trent entered the school yard. Trent yelled at Manson to leave his brother alone, and when Manson didn't move away, Trent hit him with a rock.

"A rock?" Tom's voice rose with relief. "That's what all this is about? A kid throwing a rock? Jeffrey, how many times did I heave a rock at you? It was a freak thing, right? He couldn't have known."

"He didn't throw it," Margaret said. "He'd collected it from the walk. It was big. And he brought it down on Manson's head."

"Oh, my God," Ellen said.

"Trent hasn't said a word." Margaret talking again. Tom forced himself to concentrate. "There was a lot of confusion, panic. Manson fell over. He just lay there in a pool of blood."

"Head wounds bleed." Ellen sounded desperate. "Even when they aren't serious."

Without speaking, Tom tried to send his wife a message. Shut up, Ellen. Don't say anything incriminating. Don't apologize. Don't admit.

"Can I see my boys?" Ellen asked.

My boys. Already, he was a ghost.

He followed her, of course. He went with his wife to see their children. The minute Ellen stepped through the door Alex threw his arms around her legs, sobbed into her thighs. She patted him on the back and murmured mother things. Tom stood watching, his hands twitchy and heavy on the ends of his arms. "Hey, Buddy," he managed to say, when Alex glanced up at him.

"You go with Daddy," Ellen said to Alex. He didn't want to, but in the end he relented. Tom walked with him out the door and home. Alex wouldn't hold his hand. It took them half an hour. When they got there they made hot chocolate, neither speaking, and then the chocolate got cold sitting on the table, and Tom asked Alex if he'd like to take a nap. Alex said he would. He lay down on the bottom bunk, and when Tom looked in on him fifteen minutes later, he was asleep with his thumb in his mouth. Tom watched him for a while from the doorway, then edged the door closed and stood with his forehead leaning against it.

That was nothing, though, compared to Trent. He walked in

with his mother. She had her hand on his shoulder, all Big Nurse, guiding him. His lights were out, a zombie-child who moved like a nursing home patient. Tom tried to pull his son into his arms, but Trent stood stiff as a stop sign, his head thrown aside. Tom rubbed his open hand over his mouth. Ellen walked Trent to their bed, laid him down, and covered him with a blanket. His eyes were open and staring when she closed the door.

"What's the matter with him?" he asked.

Ellen leaned back against the wall, her body sucked in and arched away from him. "Shock, partly. He'll be worse when it wears off."

"Worse," he said.

They sat up through the night, he in the den, she in the living room. He waited for Ellen to accuse him, but she didn't. She said nothing, nothing at all. They were polite when they passed each other on the way to the phone. Without talking about it, one or the other called the hospital every hour.

Late in the night, while Ellen was in the bathroom, Tom crept into the bedroom. Trent hadn't moved, his slim body stretched out like a sheeted corpse. He'd fallen asleep, his mouth slack and hanging, his breath foul and dear. Tom sat on the opposite side of the bed, afraid to touch him, afraid he'd waken.

He wished Trent had been the one hurt. No, no, not his head bashed in, not that, but the usual boyhood hurts, something of the body only, something that could heal into a scar and be shown off later in life to a girl who would laugh with him about narrow escapes and the stupidity of youth and trace the scar with her tongue, her teasing touch awakening him to hunger and love. He realized too late that he was making noise, sucking in big gasps of air. Trent rolled over and looked into his face.

"Dad?" Trent said. His voice high and young.

Tom tried to smile. "I'm here, son."

"Is Alex all right?"

Tom swallowed. "He's fine. He's sleeping in his bed."

"I tried to be a fireman."

Tom nodded, but his lips would not shape consonants. He was afraid that if he opened his mouth, he would start to howl. He muttered something like a groan, but it seemed to quiet Trent. The boy closed his eyes, turned on his side, and fell like a weighted anchor back into sleep.

Still later, after Ellen had fallen into a fitful sleep on the couch, Tom walked over to the hospital. He didn't know what he would do once he got there. He saw only one couple in the waiting room. They looked beat down, the woman frowsy and glassy-eyed, her hair thin, dry, and spiked like cactus. She wore a short-sleeved shirt, her elbows sharpened to knobby points. A man sat beside her on a chair tipped back against the wall.

His belly hung over a silver belt buckle of Mount Rushmore. He wore jeans and a plaid collared shirt, wire-rimmed glasses. He looked bookish and tough and like he could beat the crap out of Tom.

Tom peered up and down the halls but saw only a metal cart missing one caster and listed sideways. Looking for punishment, he sat down on a molded plastic chair and leaned forward, elbows on knees. "You Manson's folks?"

Expecting anger, reproof, he was unprepared for the way the woman brightened. "D'you know Manson?"

Tom shook his head. He couldn't give Trent up to these people. "No, no. I heard . . . how's he doing?"

"Twenty-seven stitches. And a concussion." The woman's voice swam in horrified awe.

"A kid did this to him," the man said. He fisted his hands on his thighs. Big hands and hard, like knots of wood.

"But he'll be all right?" Tom said.

"Doc's checking on him," the woman said.

Tom raised one trembling hand and stroked his jaw. "Helluva deal," he managed to say.

"Another boy . . . he used a rock. Why would he do that?" The woman's eyes, red-rimmed, bore into him. Tom inspected his shoes, fixed his attention on a jagged tear in the carpet.

The man dropped the chair legs to the floor. Tom winced, but the guy with big fists only leaned into Tom's face and spoke, man to man. "You know how it is. New kid in town. He's always the target."

"Hold on," Tom said. He straightened his back along the wall, the desire to confess urgent.

"I told Manson, he's got to protect himself." The man's voice rose in a whine, a tornado gathering momentum.

"He's not that kind of boy," the woman said. She lifted one side of her mouth, a twisted tooth gleaming. Tom could see the image she held of her son, doe-eyed, feeding bits of bread to ducks. Climbing into bed between cowboy sheets.

"You got kids, Mister?" the man asked.

"Yeah. Two."

"Boys?"

Tom squirmed. "Yeah."

The man opened and closed his hands, his fingers red and battered and mottled like sausages. "How do you stand it?"

"What do you mean?"

"People aren't nice. You have to teach your kids not to be nice. If you don't, they get hurt." He stopped and gestured down the hall, too choked up to go on. While Tom tried to think of something to say, the man stood abruptly, walked down the hall, and out of the hospital.

"He's gone," the woman said.

"No. He, uh, he just stepped out. He needs some air."

She smiled that crooked smile again. "He goes. He'll be gone a month, maybe two."

"A month?"

"Last time it was six."

Tom looked down the hall, anything to get away from this woman's sad eyes. "Do you want me to get him back?"

She shook her head. "Won't be no use."

The doctor beckoned from the doorway, and the woman stood and stepped into her son's room. Tom sat and stared down the empty hallway, seeing the listing cart leaned into a wall, the tear in the carpet under his shoe, everything broken, and then that stringy red-haired kid who flailed a bat at a car.

Tom left the hospital and walked a few blocks in the night to clear his head. He wandered into the city park and sat down on a rubber swing. The metal S-hooks cut into his thighs. He rocked himself back and forth and thought of Manson's father and the open road. He pictured himself alone in a bar, in a dingy motel room, in his car on a highway in Montana driving 110 miles an hour into a flat horizon with nothing more weighing on him than where he might stop to refuel. Just get in his car and go. He could. He closed his eyes and tasted freedom like acid in his mouth. Eventually he wore himself out thrashing about, and he turned his face toward the house where his wife and sons lay sleeping, warm and vulnerable. He remembered to breathe, in and then out, not so hard, and he stilled to the rhythm. Morning light began to break, and then there was nothing left but to let his feet lead him home.

DON'T CALL ME KID

Jason enjoyed the thought of disappointing his father. All week he rehearsed the moment when his dad would drive up in his big Jeep Cherokee, and Jason would flatly announce, "I'm not going." Why should he help his father relive some Wild West fantasy that had nothing to do with him? He laid on the busted chaise longue in his backyard in Des Moines, dragged his fingers through the too-long grass. He was fifteen, on summer vacation, and he let his dreams carry him. On Tuesday, he imagined his father's face elongated in surprise. On Wednesday, he heard his dad's voice quiver with rage. On Thursday, all he saw of his father were his hands gripped on the steering wheel. On Friday, Jason got out of bed early and looked in the mirror. Schmuck, he said. And then he began to pack.

"That all you're taking?" Dave asked, when he pulled into the driveway. Jason sat on the front step, a backpack at his feet. Sticking up out of it were his sketchpad and two books he was currently reading, *The Catcher in the Rye* and *The End of Nature*.

"What else do I need?" Jason didn't get up. He didn't look at his dad. He scuffed his Birkenstock sandal against the sidewalk and pushed his John Lennon rimless glasses up on his nose. He wore a tattered Grateful Dead T-shirt and cutoffs. "You got the big gun, don't you?"

"I hope you brought some long pants. You'll need them for riding."

Jason didn't answer, just heaved his pack into the rear seat of the black Jeep and climbed into the front. He looked over at his dad and stifled a laugh. Dave had exchanged his stockbroker image for the Marlboro man: tight Levi's, white yoked shirt with pearl inlaid snaps, snakeskin cowboy boots. His belly was shelved on a belt buckle the size of Rhode Island. Jason glanced in the backseat; sure enough, there was a cowboy hat, black with a pheasant feather sticking up from the band.

"Don't you think you're going to be hot? It's July. Must be a hundred degrees."

"That's why you wear this stuff." Dave sped across two lanes of traffic. "To keep the sun off."

"Mom sent sunscreen," Jason said.

Before they got outside the city limits, Dave had laid out his plans for the trip. They were on a buffalo hunt. He'd set it all up from his bachelor apartment. He called Cabela's, a big Western store out in Sidney where Nebraska bumps into Colorado. A guy named Shorty knew a rancher down by Lewellen who had wild buffalo on his rangeland.

"I drove over yesterday from Chicago," Dave said. "I'd have called you, but I figured you were busy."

"Yeah," Jason said.

They rode in silence. Interstate 80 stretched out like film off a reel. Jason stuck the earphones that hung around his neck into his ears and tuned into his music. He liked the old masters, Coltrane and Davis, guys he was sure his dad had never heard of. His dad had lived through the Sixties without even changing his hairstyle. Once, when Jason asked him how come he hadn't paid attention to Dylan or the Stones or the Dead, his dad said he guessed he'd listened to the wrong radio stations. "Besides," he said, as Jason should have known he would, "I had to work my way through school."

Eventually Dave tapped on Jason's arm to get his attention. "Why don't you park that thing?" He motioned to Jason's Walkman and hitched his thumb toward the backseat.

Jason took off the earphones, but let them rest in his lap. He turned to look out the window. Miles and miles of cornfields. A few trees sheltering scattered farmhouses. All the way from Omaha to the panhandle, where his dad was from, the road stretched flat and endless, a line extending into nothing. There were no traces of the family left out there. His dad had taken him to Reach once when he was younger. Jason's parents were still married then, and they'd stayed together in the downtown Deluxe Motel, six ramshackle side-by-side units. A sign in the manager's office boasted of running water and TV in every room. "This is where I grew up, Son," his dad had said. "This is the town that made a man out of me."

Dave drummed his fingers on the steering wheel. After a few more miles, he cleared his throat. "How's your mother?"

"Mom's fine." Neither turned their heads away from the road in front of them.

"Thought maybe she'd say hello this morning."

Sometimes Jason couldn't believe his father. Where he got off. "She was at work."

Dave flipped a cigarette pack out of his shirt pocket. With practiced moves, he tucked a Marlboro between his lips, found the lighter in the bin between the seats, lit the cigarette, and slid the package home. He was blowing out the first puff as Jason rolled down his window.

"I got the air on," Dave said.

"Yeah, well, you're contaminating it." The wind blew his longish blond hair across his face. One end caught the corner of his mouth; another smacked his eye. Still, he kept his window down.

Dave took two more long draws. "Shit." Dave stubbed out his

cigarette in the ashtray. "In my day, it was the kids who smoked, and the parents who told them not to."

"Maybe we're smarter now."

"Than what?"

Jason shrugged his shoulders. Rolled up the window.

"Smarter now than then or smarter than your parents? Which is it?"

Jason did not answer. He knew his dad in this mood.

"Let me tell you something, kid. You don't know everything. And you're not the first kid who thought he did."

They rode a few more miles in silence. Then, without turning his head, Jason said, "Don't call me kid."

They stopped in Grand Island for gas, Kearney for lunch at McDonald's. Dave ordered a Big Mac Meal Deal, dipped his French fries first in mayonnaise, then ketchup. Jason had a salad and chicken nuggets, no sauce.

Once they were headed west again, driving straight into the amber sun, Jason took out *The Catcher in the Rye*.

"I read that," Dave said.

"What'd you think?"

Dave shrugged. "Don't remember much about it. Except it's about a kid who's kind of lost."

Jason thumbed down the page corner. "Holden Caulfield."

"What?"

"The kid you think was lost. His name is Holden Caulfield."

"Yeah, I guess that's right."

"Except it's the culture that's lost."

"Huh?"

"That's the point. Of the book."

Dave didn't say anything for a mile or two. "It's not normal," he finally said.

Jason grunted, hoping his dad would shut the fuck up.

"The way you see things. You're kind of twisted."

Jason squinted, pictured an eagle in flight, soaring, soaring, up and away.

"Not that it's your fault."

"Leave Mom alone." He made his voice hard, flinty.

After a few more miles, Dave said, "Remember that time we went on that baseball tour?"

Jason looked up from his book. It was two years after his father walked out on them. Jason was eleven, and they'd gone on a whirlwind tour of major league baseball games. Each night in a different motel room identical to the one from the night before, reeking of cigarettes and chlorine, Jason endured a quiz. He recited players' names, ERAS, and analyzed what went wrong on second base in the third inning. He kept the baseball cards stuffed in his bottom desk drawer, hidden under snapshots and debris. Every time he chanced upon them, he knew he should throw them away. But then he'd remember hot dogs and pretzels and sitting by his dad, and he couldn't bring himself to do it.

Now he said, "Not really."

"You had your nose in a book most of that whole trip," Dave said.

Jason shifted in his seat. His legs seemed to have gotten too long for the car, and he didn't know what to do with his elbows. The air in the Jeep felt close, clammy on his skin. He actually put his palm on the roof over his head, as if he might shove the top open and find some relief.

Jason dropped Holden Caulfield on the floor and reached for his sketchpad. With quick strokes of a soft-leaded pencil, he drew a boxy car, high-wheeled. He drew a sun, oversized and glaring, and a long, white ribbon of road. Sticking out the windows of the boxy car, he drew twigs. They jutted and poked at crazy angles, twisted one over another, completely jammed the car. Then, he turned the twigs into French fries, the ends drenched with drippings. He added spokes to the high wheels, and between the spokes, he inserted chrome emblems that looked something like baseball cards. His father might have said something to him, or he might not. Jason was out of reach.

The farther they went across Nebraska, the longer the road seemed to get. It stretched like taffy, like time when there's nothing to do. They decided to stay overnight in Ogallala. Dave pulled up to a Super 8 along the interstate. They had supper across the viaduct in a tourist trap called Front Street: saloon with swinging doors, red lights, sawdust on a wood floor, honky-tonk piano player, and a menu that offered beef or buffalo. In one corner, on a raised stage, a poker game was shrouded in heavy smoke. Satin-and-lace women draped over the arms of fringe-vested men wearing holsters and chaps. Jason looked at the crowd and tried to guess which were tourists and which were locals. Some of the men looked tanned and leathery, some were even bowlegged. But then, Jason knew most modern ranchers drove sports vehicles and sat around in computerized offices. For all he knew, the guys in the crowd who looked like real cowboys might be actors. Or stockbrokers in disguise like his dad.

Dave plopped his beer down on the table, sloshing the foam over the side. "I'd buy you one, kid, but I don't want to get arrested." He set a root beer in front of Jason, frosty mug.

Dave lowered himself to the straight-backed chair, stuck one booted leg out in front of him, tipped the chair back on its heels. "You're probably the only guy in here wearing an earring."

Jason tossed his head to lift a blond wave off his eye.

"What's next? A tattoo?"

Jason felt Dave looking at him. He wanted something from him, Jason didn't know what. He picked up his mug of root beer. He'd have preferred a Coke. His dad—fake costume, fake beer.

The fake poker game over in the corner was heating up to a staged gunfight. Pretty soon they'd be caught in a fake crossfire.

"Look at that big guy." Dave pointed to a mounted buffalo head that loomed over the bar. "Once king of the prairie. Here's to you, you poor sonofabitch." Dave lifted his glass to the buffalo and drank.

Jason wished his dad would just eat so he could get out of here. He felt sick to his stomach. One of the cowboys in the poker game accused another one of cheating.

"My dad was one of those guys who couldn't adapt. Happy growing sugar beets on a few acres, then the war came along. After that, the name of the game was progress." He rapped his knuckles on the table. "Can't accommodate, you're obsolete."

Jason said nothing. He'd heard this sob story before.

Dave took a swig of beer, ran his tongue over his lips. He gazed into the glass eyes of the buffalo. "I was just about your age, full of myself." He paused. "Told my mother that if I ever had kids and couldn't provide a decent living, I hoped somebody'd take a shotgun to my head. I was quite the little hard-ass."

Jason thought about the checks his mom got every month in the mail. Maybe they bought his dad peace of mind, but they didn't mean squat. He dropped his buffalo burger into the red plastic basket and shoved it across the table. "I can't eat this stuff," he said. The basket collided with his dad's beer, then dangled precariously on the edge of the table before falling to the floor.

Dave leaned his head forward and surveyed the damage. He picked up his beer and raised it to his lips. Holding the beer suspended, he looked at Jason. "Suit yourself," he said.

After supper, Dave insisted that they drive ten miles north to the Kingsley Dam. The landscape shifted as they moved out of the town limits. Cornfields gave way to yuccas and sage. The air was drier, the sun more insistent, the trees huddled around low places or watering troughs. In the distance Jason spotted a lone windmill keeping vigil on the prairie.

"I remember fishing in Lake McConaughy," Dave said, driving north. "One time, our whole family went. Camped out right on the sand. White bass every time we threw in the line. We must've hit a school. Caught so many we ran out of bait. Mom had a couple shiny buttons, so we tried those. Worked just like a minnow. Dad decided we should use fish eyes. Damned if they didn't strike at those. A guy up around the bend wasn't catching a thing, yelled at us, wanted to know what we were using for bait. I asked Dad what I should say. He said, 'Tell them the truth, Son.' So I yelled back, 'Fish eyes.'" Dave snorted. "'Course the guy didn't believe me. Let out a blue streak."

Jason was silent. He was thinking about fish eyes, iridescent silver and green. He saw the empty sockets of the eyeless, dying fish.

They stretched their legs by walking across the dam. The lake itself was narrow and twenty-six miles long, east to west. The sun squatted low on the horizon, orange and coral fanned above it like a peacock's tail. Buttons of color shimmered in the sun-streaked water. Along the shoreline sprouted pockets of willow trees, here and there a cottonwood. Cattails waved in the marshes. Jason and his dad stood and propped their arms on the railing.

"Beautiful," Dave said.

"Nobody fishes with fish eyes," Jason said.

After breakfast next morning, they set out to find the ranch. Jason wore his jeans, a T-shirt, and tennis shoes. His dad wore his Western regalia with a clean red plaid shirt. They drove to Lewellen, all the way around the south side of the lake, its waters glistening now and then through a gap in the hills. They passed Ash Hollow and Windlass Hill. Dave told Jason a lot of pioneers died there until they figured out a pulley system to get their wagons safely up and over the ridge. They went past a hillside cemetery, boots upside down on every fencepost.

"What's that for?"

"Pointing home," Dave said.

When they got to Lewellen, they couldn't find the cutoff to the Porter Ranch. Dave circled through the three-block town, then turned back and circled again.

"There's a gas station back there," Jason said.

"It's got to be here," Dave said. "I know Shorty said out of Lewellen."

Dave U-turned the Jeep to make another swipe through town.

"Dad, it's not here. Why don't you stop and ask?"

"Don't tell me how to drive. This is my car and my trip."

Jason pushed down on the door handle. The door flew open. Even though they were moving slowly, a gust of air caused the car to careen to the side. Dave lurched the Jeep to a halt in the gravel alongside the gas station. "What the hell is the matter with you?" Dave shouted.

Jason already had one leg out the door. By the time Dave followed him into the gas station, Jason had gotten directions from the attendant. Turns out the ranch wasn't exactly out of Lewellen.

"Let me see the map," Jason said, when they got back to the Jeep.

"You heard the guy. Porter Ranch is out of Arthur, and Arthur is north of the other end of the lake. We'll have to go all the way back." Still, Dave waited until Jason had wrestled open the map.

"There's a different road around the north side," Jason said, his finger pointing at the map. "It's closer."

"I forgot about that road," Dave said, leaning over. Jason could feel his dad's breath on his face. "Goes right through Lemoyne. Don't blink or you'll miss it."

By now, the weekend traffic had picked up. Progress was slow because the road was narrow and hilly, crammed with campers and pickup trucks.

"Christ," Dave said. "We'll be lucky to get there by noon." He thumped his hand on the steering wheel, took chances passing, dove in and out of the traffic. Jason hung on to the dashboard with one hand.

"My dad used to drive us out in these parts. There's a town north of Arthur, way up there in the Sandhills, where several millionaires lived. Hyannis, I think it's called."

Jason tried to picture his dad as a boy, thumping along in the backseat of some washed-out Chevy. "What was your dad like?"

Dave did not take his eyes off the road. "Stubborn. And weak." Dave snorted. "Now that, right there, is a lethal combination."

They made it to the Porter Ranch by 10:00 a.m. Shorty was waiting for them. He'd driven down from Cabela's to make sure the transaction went smoothly.

Shorty wore jeans and a short-sleeved shirt, boots. After shaking their hands, guffawing, pats on the back all around, Shorty introduced them to the other two guys. Leo, the owner of the ranch, may have had some Indian blood in him; he had the coloring and high cheekbones. Amos, Leo's friend, was tall and lean, like Jimmy Stewart in *My Darling Clementine*. Jason guessed he was the oldest of the three, maybe in his sixties. Amos lifted his dad's rifle out of the back of the Jeep and spoke in a slow Southern drawl.

"Nice little piece you got here."

"It was my dad's," Dave answered. "He used to hunt deer with it." Dave was buckling on a bandolier that held rifle shells. The brass casings glistened in the hot sun.

"I reckon it'll take down a buffalo, all right." Amos handed the rifle to Dave.

"Shorty," Leo instructed. "Take these two cowboys out to the barn and get them acquainted with their horses. Amos and I are going up to the house to get the packs."

"Do you know how to ride, Son?" Shorty asked Jason, as they trailed him to the barn.

"Sure he does," Dave answered, clapping Jason on the shoulder.

Jason had been on a horse before, trail rides and scout camp, but he'd never ridden a range horse across open country. He shrugged off his father's hand. "I guess so," Jason said to Shorty.

"We'll give you Frieda here." Shorty pointed out a roan-colored mare. "She's as good as they come."

"How about you?" Shorty said to Dave. "Ride?"

"Hell, yes," Dave said. "Been a while, but it's like riding a bicycle, right?"

Shorty saddled up Frieda for Jason and then helped Dave with Billy, a gray gelding with a long sloping back.

"Is there a bathroom somewhere?" Jason asked. "Before we head out?"

"Sure, Son," Shorty said. "Go on up to the house."

Jason made his way toward the low ranch house. On the way back, he rounded the corner of the barn. Amos and Leo were saddling their horses in the shade of the overhang.

"Christ," Leo said. "I damn near forgot the camera. Shorty said be sure to bring it, they always want a trophy picture."

Jason stopped, embarrassed at overhearing them.

"Where'd Shorty come up with this guy, anyway?" Amos asked.

"Says he called Cabela's, some rich banker or something out of Chicago. Wanted to take his kid on a buffalo hunt. I been needing to get rid of that old bull. Somebody wants to pay me $1,500 for the privilege of shooting him, saves me the trouble of carting him off to the slaughterhouse."

"I hope he stays put in that draw until we get there," Amos said. "Otherwise we'll have a real hunt on our hands."

"Hell," Leo said. "He's too old to go anywhere else. I'm surprised he didn't just lay down and die when we drove him out there this morning."

The two men laughed. Jason kicked himself into motion. He cleared his throat and moved forward. "Just on my way back from the house," Jason said. He walked straight past them, not even glancing their way. He didn't realize until he was standing in the barn that he was holding his breath. He let it out in a jagged sigh. His dad and Shorty were already mounted so there was nothing to do but put his foot in the stirrup, heft himself into the saddle, and ride out.

They trotted around the ranch for the rest of the morning. Dave was in high spirits, pointing out the call of meadowlarks, prairie dog mounds, termites housed under cow pies flipped over by the horses' hooves. He talked genially with the other men and worked hard to include Jason. Jason rode on the edges and refused to say much. His eyes were on the prairie, on the gray sage and knife-bladed yucca, the sparse grass brown from the summer sun. Dust clogged his nostrils, gnats swarmed around his ears. He heard the saddle creak with every move of his body. The heat hung in shimmering waves, distorting the view like a funhouse mirror.

They stopped at lunchtime beside a windmill and a watering trough for the horses. A small stand of cottonwoods skirted the tank, and Dave demonstrated how to fold a leaf to make a whistle. "My dad could play 'Yankee Doodle' on a cottonwood leaf," he said.

"Your dad take you hunting?" Amos said, as he and Leo handed out cold beef sandwiches, potato chips, and lemonade.

"Ducks and pheasants, mostly," Dave said. "I was pretty young. Haven't hunted much since then."

"You're lucky," Amos said to Dave. He looked over at Jason and nodded. "My dad run off before I was born."

"I never thought much about it at the time. Just hunting, my old man, what he did."

"Wait," Jason burst in. His insides roiled. He couldn't stand watching his dad being played by these cowpokes.

"What's the matter, Jason?" Dave said. They all turned and looked at him. His dad's face filled with concern. Jason rocked from one foot to another.

"Dad, can I talk to you alone a minute?"

"Can't it wait?" Dave motioned vaguely to the other men. They were comrades now. Jason would never get his dad away from them.

"It's about . . . it's about the hunt." Jason saw Amos and Leo look at each other.

"Well, let's hear it. We don't have any secrets here," Dave said.

"I think we should turn around and go back," Jason said.

Jason felt his dad probing deep into his eyes. For a minute, he thought his dad might actually listen to him. Dave turned to the other men.

"I think he's getting cold feet, what do you gentlemen think?" They all chuckled. Leo and Amos scuffed at the ground with the toes of their boots. Shorty reached up and rubbed his hand along the line of his jaw. Jason turned away from their laughing faces. He drained his lemonade onto the parched ground and crumpled the paper cup into his hand. The edges of the cup bit into his palm and without flinching, he squeezed tighter.

They saddled up and rode on, up and over the range, in circles, what difference did it make? Jason couldn't stand to look at his father. He could feel Amos, Leo, and Shorty sneering at them behind their backs. The heat clamped down on him. He couldn't see the land, his eyes were glazed and inward, and the men left him alone. He wished his father would hurry up, get this day over with.

Mid-afternoon, they found the buffalo. He was standing within a short draw, the banks so shallow they offered no shade. A big clump of sage partially blocked the entrance, otherwise the buffalo stood in plain sight. The men began to whisper and move in slow motion, as if they were stalking a dangerous lion. The old buffalo watched them with mournful eyes, his head hanging heavy and low. Dave motioned for Jason to walk next to him. When they were less than fifty yards away, Dave knelt and yanked Jason down beside him. Jason looked at the dirt and tensed his body. He heard his dad load the shell into the big 270 and lock the bolt into place. He waited while Dave aimed the rifle and pulled the trigger. The shot reverberated in the open air, riding on the waves of heat, and Jason heard his dad say, "I'll be damned." Jason raised his eyes, prepared to face the staggering beast, and realized that his father had missed the shot. The buffalo, magnificent in his size and dignified in his presence, stood looking at them calmly.

Dave's mouth hung slack, his eyes unblinking, surprise carved into his face. He shook his head from side to side as if to clear it.

"Here," Dave said, shoving the rifle at Jason. "You try."

Jason nearly dropped the rifle. "No, Dad." He whispered it, a loud stage whisper. "I don't want to."

"Go on. It's your chance."

Jason looked at his father. How could anyone miss that shot? His dad was being played for a fool, but was his dad playing him? His dad's face showed nothing, blank and bewildered.

Jason looked at the faces of the other men, waiting and watching him expectantly. What were they thinking? That he was just a kid, afraid to take a shot? That his dad was so lame that his own son wouldn't follow him? He moved his eyes from face to face, looking for something, wanting somebody to help him, knowing it was impossible, and when he reached Amos, the man slowly nodded. "Go ahead, Son," he said softly. "Can't hurt anything."

Jason took up the weapon in his hands. The wood felt smooth and warm under his palms. He watched himself load the shell, heard the bolt drop in place like a heavy cellar door. He looked down the barrel and sighted between the eyes of the buffalo. He squeezed the trigger. The buffalo dropped without a shudder. The men whooped and pounded Jason on the back. They rushed forward, even his dad, while Jason stood up, the rifle slack in his arms, his mind struggling with what he had done.

Jason's ears rang. He felt weak-kneed and thought he might swoon. His dad motioned for him to come and stand beside him. "Bring the rifle," Dave called, his voice ringing with pride. Dave crouched in front of the buffalo's carcass, the flanks of the huge animal forming a dark backdrop.

"No, no, the other side," Leo said, looking through the lens of his camera. "You'll want the head," and he motioned to Dave to come around.

Jason stepped into the camera's range. He felt his dad's arm go around him. He mopped his face with his shirtsleeve. He slipped his arm around his dad's back, hooked his fingers over his shoulder. A meadowlark's somber voice rode through the stillness, and Jason cocked his ear to it. The heat draped around him like a veil as he lifted his head for the shot.

THE SKY IS FALLING

Buck was asleep when Ella woke him to tell him she'd been saved at the revival meeting. She sat on the edge of their four-poster bed, her hip snugged against his, her smooth hand on his cheek. Her long, loose hair tickled his bare chest. He was aroused, conscious of her breasts, her waist. She smelled of new rain. He wanted her to slip off her cotton dress and lie naked with him. He reached for her, but as soon as his hands clasped her arms, she moved her palm to his chest and pushed him back down on the bed.

"Buck. Wait. Listen to me."

He shook his head to clear it of dreams, of desire. He forced himself to look into her face instead of down the front of her dress, at the slope of her lovely neck and the rise of flesh. Nipples he knew by touch and taste.

"Yeah. What?"

"I got saved tonight."

"Saved? From what?"

"Sin. Eternal fire."

"Since when are you worried about that?"

"We're all sinful. We can't help it. But if we accept Jesus, then we're cleansed."

He sat up against the headboard and rubbed his head with his hand. His sandy hair stood on end. "We don't need religion," he said.

She smiled but withdrew her hand. "Maybe you don't."

She rose from the bed and shook out of her shoes. She slid her dress off, draped it over a chair. Buck watched her move in the moonlight, hoped she'd come straight to bed without bothering with her summer nightgown, but she took it from the top dresser drawer, drew it down over her milky thighs. When she did finally slip into bed, she propped on one elbow, tapped him on the nose with her forefinger like he was a willful child, and said, "You'll find out." Then she rolled over, away from him, leaving him lying in a cold sweat.

He hadn't minded when cousin Lily asked Ella to go with her to the revival meetings in Reach. He knew Ella got bored and lonesome out here on the farm. He'd known Ella since they were kids reciting in a one-room country schoolhouse. He knew she feared spiders, that her feet were big for a woman her size, that a boy cousin once talked her out of her underpants so he could examine her (eyes only, no touching) in the haymow. He knew (and had kissed) the backs of her knees, her eyelids, run his tongue along the inside of her mouth. He knew she dreamed of far-off places, listened to Johnny Cash, once rode the Tilt-A-Whirl seven times in a row. He knew things even she didn't know, that she snored softly when she rolled onto her back, that the tip of her tongue poked out the side of her mouth when she concentrated. He could set his watch by her habits. She brought food to the field two times a day, mid-morning and mid-afternoon, and his heart stopped every time he caught her silhouette against the prairie sun. He kissed her in the coatroom when they were seven, sent her a valentine (signed xoxoxo) when they were ten, and by the time they graduated from high school, he could barely wait until she grew tired of college and agreed to marry him. What brought her home, of course, was that her mother died. By then, his people, except for cousin Lily, had moved to Wisconsin. Uncle Harold had died, leaving him this land when he was barely twenty. Ella came home to help her dad and younger siblings, but he knew—call it fate—she'd never go back.

He went to bed early because he arose early, and usually Ella got up with him, made coffee and flapjacks or scrambled eggs. The week of the revival, she slept in. She stayed up late reading the Bible, all the begats and Psalms and the Sermon on the Mount. He hadn't minded, the first day, but he missed her. Plus, his coffee was horrible. The next day, he sat at the breakfast table, gnawed on cold cereal, drank the stinking black brew, and wished his wife would come down the stairs, knowing she wouldn't. By the third day, his heart turned hard against the church and Jesus and the Twenty-third Psalm. He didn't want to hear it.

Lily picked Ella up four nights in a row, and on this fifth night, Ella came home glowing, sat on the edge of their bed, and announced she'd been saved. She'd walked down the aisle to an altar call while the congregants sang "I Need Thee Every Hour," and lying awake long after Ella had fallen into sleep, Buck realized that her taking up with the Lord Jesus was as bad as if she had a lover stashed behind the barn.

He refused to go with her to church on Sundays. Lily and John picked her up, their kids waving from the backseat of their spanking-new Impala. He thought once the revivals were over, Ella would give it up, but no, she had to go to regular church. Reverend Kane was the Baptist minister, and she thought he walked on water right next to Jesus.

He had loved their Sundays best of all, waking up slow. Sometimes they made love before they got out of bed. Ella cooked what she called brunch, a big breakfast meal late in the morning, fried potatoes and eggs, crackling bacon, a fruit salad, cinnamon rolls or toasted home-baked bread. They lounged, walked through the day in bare feet. Sometimes they sat outside on the porch and listened to the radio. Although the talk was all Cold War and Communism, Sputnik orbiting unseen around the earth, nothing threatened them. Not here. Occasionally her dad or one of the neighbors stopped by in the afternoon. Over coffee and Ella's gingerbread cookies, they laughed and told stories, and he felt pride in all that was his, this land, a good woman.

All that was ruined when Ella got saved. She rushed him through an early breakfast. The minute her coffee was drunk, she dashed upstairs to put on her Sunday best, nylon stockings and heels, one of the two dresses she wore to town. She bussed him on the cheek while running out the door. He spent the morning in anguish, furious at being abandoned. They ate leftovers for lunch. She used the afternoon to cook a fine meal for supper, but he ate it with bitterness. Tired and distant, they went to bed.

He endured this for four Sundays and then decided to put his foot down. He'd read the Bible, some. His parents had taken him to a Methodist Sunday School before a scandal involving the preacher and one of the deacon's wives had soured them. He decided to take the matter up after lunch on Saturday. He cleared his throat. She was already starting the dishes. Not wanting to appear domineering, he sat at the table.

"Ella, I don't want you going to church on Sundays." There, it was out. Simple and clear.

She turned, her hands soapy. Her face white. Ashen, really. It pained him to look at it. Still, he knew this was best for both of them.

"Well, Buck, I don't think that's up to you."

He was surprised at her tone. At her resistance. But then again, he'd planned for it. He forced himself to look in her face. He wished now he'd stood, since it'd be easier to be stern if he was looking down at her, but it felt awkward getting up at this point.

Instead, he reached for the coffeepot and slowly refilled his cup. When coffee was at the brim, he stopped and set the pot down. All this time, she waited. He thought that was good, to keep her waiting, on pins and needles for his response.

"I know what the Bible says. It says wives are to be submissive to their husbands." He stirred sugar into his coffee.

She laughed. Laughed! "Oh Buck, you're not going to try that, are you? That's not you."

Her laughter infuriated him. He stood then. Heat flamed his face. "I mean it. I forbid you to go."

"Why?"

Why? He hadn't expected that. Why should he have to explain? Because. Because he said so. But she stood there, her face open and lovely. He felt his hands reach out independent of his mind, turn up pleading. "Well, because I want . . . I want you here."

"Oh, Buck." She dried her hands on the towel wrapped round her waist. She walked across the room, rose on her tiptoes, and kissed him. "I am here. I love you. I can, you know. I can love you and want to go to church." All this time, she nuzzled his ear, kissed his cheek and throat. He couldn't think because his hands were busy exploring her body. "Come with me tomorrow."

He shook his head no. No, he couldn't. He wouldn't. But then he forgot the argument entirely because she led him to the living room couch and ministered to him with her flesh, and everything felt all right again, though he knew, somewhere deep inside, that whole tectonic plates had shifted.

He set out to win her back. He strategized. Mounted a campaign. He couldn't forbid her to go to church without losing her trust in him. He could see that. Maybe it worked for other men, but he didn't want to order Ella to do the things he loved. He wanted her to want to please him. He wanted things to be the way they were before she got into all this religious nonsense.

"Tell me about being saved." He said this over supper, fried chicken and green beans. He'd brought zinnias in from the garden, cut the stems himself, placed them in the blue glass vase that had belonged to her mother. He washed up before he kissed her, laced his arms around her from behind, his lips low on her neck. She swatted him playfully, nothing new in that, but he found he scrutinized her responses in a way he'd never done before. Did she sigh when he moved toward her in their bed? Did she close her eyes while they kissed so she could imagine being somewhere else?

She leaned toward him across the table. He fell into her eyes like a fly into beer batter. "It's not like you think."

"How do you know what I think?" He heard the defensiveness in his voice, tried to soften it with a smile.

She swept her hair and tucked it behind one ear. "It's not about guilt and fear, like you said." (He had said that once, in a fit of anger, a tactic that had not worked.)

"Okay. What is it about?"

"Belonging. Love. Being part of a community."

He fidgeted in his chair. Worse than he thought. "But you belong here. I love you."

She patted his hand. He felt five years old. He wanted to slap her. "I know. But this is different. This is being part of something bigger."

He narrowed his eyes. She needed to have a child. He could see that now. He'd wanted to wait until they were more on their feet. Also (he'd never admit this to her), he wasn't ready to share her. He'd seen what happened to his friends, their wives suddenly turned into mothers. Sex, if they got any, scheduled between feedings.

"I've been thinking." He reached his hand out to her face, traced his finger along her cheek. "Maybe it's time for a baby."

She recoiled. "You think that's what this is about? Having a baby will fix everything?"

"What do you mean, everything?"

She stood. Slammed dishes on the counter. When she turned, her hands were braced behind her. "I'm not ready for a baby. Not now. Maybe, I don't know, maybe never."

"What?" He knew she wanted children. They'd never talked about it. All women wanted children, didn't they?

She waved her arms around, flailed them. Wild. He'd never seen her like this. Her face was red and, well, swollen.

"I spent my childhood taking care of my brothers and sisters. I don't think I had a childhood. At all. I never . . . I just don't want to think about that right now. I don't . . . I can't . . ."

"Okay. Okay." He held his hands out, palms down, gentling her as if she were a cornered animal. What had gotten into her? He backed away, bumped his leg into the chair. "Guess I'll go on out, check the irrigation."

Next morning, after they'd shared a nearly silent breakfast, she handed him a brown paper bag, folded at the top. In her other hand, a thermos. "There's hot coffee. And I packed you a snack."

"You're not coming out to the field?"

"Lily's coming by this morning. We're working on a sewing project for the Women's Mission Society."

She must have read the look on his face, because she quickly added. "Don't worry. I'll have your lunch on the table when you come in."

Never before had the phrase—struck dumb—made so much sense to him. What could he possibly say? That he didn't care about zucchini bread or fruit tarts or whatever the hell she packed in there. He'd made a point to praise her mid-morning offerings. He wasn't an idiot. He wanted her to come out to the field. He wanted her, the sight of her, the knowledge of her. To go a whole morning not seeing her felt like punishment, and what had he done to deserve this?

He felt his jaw go taut. He knew the stern look that inhabited his face; he'd seen it enough times on his father's. He wanted to smack down her God, lay waste to whole cities. He turned on his heel and left the room, knowing full well he'd fume throughout the morning and God in heaven (or whoever, wherever), he didn't know how they'd get through lunch.

He needn't have worried. By the time he got back to the house, Lily's car was gone. He walked in the back door, smelled frying pork chops, washed up at the lavatory off the kitchen. He could hear Ella humming but didn't recognize the tune. Ella met him fresh eyed and all smiles. She kissed him on the mouth. He was relieved. Of course he was, but what the hell? How could she send him off like that and pretend everything was peachy-dandy?

He sat down in his usual place. He tried to be patient while she bowed her head and said her little prayer, her lips moving silently. When she looked up, she beamed at him. He was puzzled by it, felt the furrow in his brow.

"How was your morning, Buck?"

She handed him bowls of food. He dished up pork chops, peppery and brown, creamy mashed potatoes, gravy without a lump. After that, peas from their garden, a cucumber salad.

"Fine. Got the tubes set in the east cornfield. Beans look dry, too."

She nodded. He fell silent, busy forking food into his mouth. He noticed she wasn't eating much. Before second helpings, he asked, "How was Lily?"

"Oh, she was fine. We didn't work too long, only about an hour. She brought strawberries. I had time to make that pie you like so much."

He felt the hairs on the back of his neck stir. He got this feeling sometimes before a big storm, when the sky was still blue and not yet darkened.

"Is that so?"

"Buck, I want to be baptized."

Not good. Not good. They're getting their hooks in deeper. "Do you think that's a good idea?"

"I want to be baptized, and I want it to be here, on our land. In our pond. I already talked to Reverend Kane, and he said it was all right with him."

"You offered our pond, without asking me?" He was biding for time. His thoughts racing. Should he be outraged? Should he refuse? If he went along with this, would it seem like he was condoning this whole religious debacle? Or, would it be a good thing, earn her trust, let her know he's capable of supporting her? She'd likely do it anyway. Wouldn't it be better if he made himself part of it?

"I'm asking you now."

Buck jerked his attention back to Ella. He'd nearly forgotten the strain of the conversation; he'd been so busy with his own thoughts. He studied her face, on watch for signs of wile, manipulation. Was she using him? Mocking him? She looked like she always did, radiant and beautiful. Her lips were slightly parted, and he thought about kissing her when more words flowed out.

"It would make it special to me. To have it here. On our own place. Lily said she'd help with the food."

"Food?" He knew he sounded like an idiot. He *was* an idiot. Why couldn't he muster a coherent thought?

"Some of the congregation will come. We figured about twenty-five or thirty people. We thought it could be on a Saturday. Maybe in the morning. We'd do it potluck, and Lily said she'd help. You wouldn't have to do a thing."

He squirmed, uncomfortable. Twenty-five or thirty people. Why, where would they sit? And that pond was nothing but a glorified mudhole. He'd have to line the bottom with rocks or it wouldn't hold a person's weight.

"When?"

He heard Ella take a big breath. She looked excited, the way he always thought a son or daughter might look on Christmas morning. "August 28."

He frowned. "That's your birthday."

"I know. Isn't that perfect?"

Too much. This whole thing really was too damn much. He didn't want to share his wife's birthday with a bunch of pious Bible-thumping strangers. He didn't want them swarming all over his land, tromping on his pasture on the way down to that pond. That date was six weeks away, and by then the pond could be dried up. He latched on to that last thought. Likely, the pond would be dried up. He could agree to this and not have to go through with it. Besides, in four, five weeks, Ella might be over this infatuation. He had come to think of it as an infection, something she got exposed to that had to run its course. Not her fault so much as a sickness to be endured with compassion and forbearance.

"All right." He heard the words before he had consciously shaped them. Ella heard them, too. She clapped her hands together, stood to bring him that strawberry pie, the top swirled with whipped cream. She looked happy, and that hurt most of all. The idea that he was making his wife happy by helping her cuckold him!

That wasn't the only inconsistency in Buck's life that summer. Whoever heard of a farmer praying that it wouldn't rain? He wouldn't call it prayer, but his hopes were set on that pond drying up. Instead, the skies opened weekly, on schedule. His crops never looked better. The prairie grass grew so lush, he'd have to mow a path down to that pond. Ella showed no signs of loosening up on her zeal. If anything, she was more intent, spending any spare time she had sewing herself a baptismal gown, the fabric floaty and white. When she showed him, he said, "What are you wearing under it?"

She blushed. "Why, Buck? I'll be wearing a slip, of course. All my usual underthings."

He grabbed the edge of the table and forced himself to say nothing, picturing her emerging from the pond, soaked, that white dress plastered to her curved body. He thought he might have to put his head down between his knees, the temptation to slip out of this world coming over him strong.

Then, two weeks before the baptism, the sky rained blackbirds. He didn't see it happen, only the aftermath. He'd gone to check on the pond, over the rise in the pasture floor, past the lone cottonwood, and literally stumbled over a dead red-winged blackbird. He'd had his mind and his eyes on the sky while he walked, judging the proximity of rain. When he looked down at the toe of his boot, he saw black-feathered bird bodies everywhere, in a swath that stretched all the way to the pond. Clustered tight, twisted and knotted, some with wings outstretched, the sight sickening and terrifying. What could he make of it? He half-ran back to the barn, grabbed some old gunnysacks and a pitchfork, loaded them in the back of the pickup. He had to make that trip twice more, each time underestimating the number of sacks required to hold the carcasses. He counted 462 dead blackbirds by the time he had recovered all of them. He wept through most of the gathering, unable to fathom what could have caused such a calamity. Was there nothing he could count on? If the bottom could fall out of the sky, what next? Water running uphill? A year without spring?

He fished 32 dead birds out of the pond, worried about contamination. From the look of the corpses, they hadn't been there long. Not days. The birds must have fallen the night before, but he'd heard nothing.

He loaded the carcasses in the back of the pickup and dumped them all in a far corner of his land where his uncle had previously chucked an old sofa and bedsprings, a kitchen range, a pile of magazines. On second thought, he picked up three of the birds by their tiny feet and dropped them back into a gunnysack, slung them in the bed of the truck.

He drove up to the house, but he couldn't face Ella. Instead, he took the coward's way out. While Ella was weeding in the garden, he sneaked into the house, left a note on the kitchen table saying he had to go to town; he'd be back soon. In a flurry, he added, *Love, Buck.*

He hopped into the pickup and sped down the lane, dust kicking up behind him and into the open windows, caking on his sweaty skin. He drove like a hypnotic, eyes on the road, mind numb, disconnected from his body. In town, he pulled up to the County Extension Office. He was in the lobby before he realized he'd left the truck. Luckily, Joe Bolden, the County Agent, was in.

"What's up, Buck? You look like you've seen a ghost."

The laughter froze on Joe's lips. Buck thought he must look truly frightful for Joe to clam up like that. Joe was known for his good humor, always a helping hand and a joke. People liked him. Farmers liked him. He wasn't from around here, came from somewhere east, maybe Ohio, but he fit in. He liked his late afternoon beer, and he had two boys who were stars on the basketball team.

Buck swallowed and tried to remember how to make his lips form words. "I found a whole mess of dead blackbirds on my land this morning."

"You don't say."

Buck nodded.

"How many?"

"Four hundred sixty-two. Scattered over that pasture close up by the house."

"Jesus."

Joe swiped his hand over his mouth, whether to erase taking the Lord's name or show his dismay, Buck didn't know. Didn't care, either. He held out the gunnysack to Joe. He wanted him to take it off his hands. He wanted Joe to tell him why.

"I thought you might want to take a look."

Joe grasped the neck of the sack but didn't peer inside. He just stared into Buck's face. Finally he shifted his weight, carefully laid the sack on his desk, rolled down the top to reveal the bird bodies. Buck winced with the sight.

"No obvious damage," Joe said.

"They're dead."

"I know that. But no burns. They can't have hit a power line. No visible signs of disease. Or pests. Were they all like this?"

Buck nodded.

"What did you do with them? The rest of them?"

Buck shrugged. "Dumped them out by the dry gulch."

"Tell you what. I'm going to call down to the university. See if they've ever heard of such a thing. Maybe they'll want me to send the bodies to a lab somewhere. But I think you better bury those birds. If they are diseased, we don't know what could happen once the coyotes get at 'em."

Buck nodded. Hell, he'd already lost a half-day of work.

"Do you know if anybody else found dead birds? Did you call Hank or any other neighbors?"

"No. I came straight here. After I picked them up. That pond, see." Buck fidgeted, bounced from foot to foot. No help for it, he had to go on and say what he'd come here to say. "Ella's being baptized in a couple of weeks. In that pond. I need to know . . . I don't want her going under that water if there's anything bad in there."

"Yeah, okay. I see what you mean."

"Then, if there isn't, well, I'd just as soon keep it quiet. Ella's counting on that day."

"Yeah. I can see that, too. We don't want everybody all stirred up over what may be nothing but a fluke of nature. Hell, maybe they all died of old age." Joe guffawed, his old humor springing out.

Buck tried to laugh, too, but for the life of him, he couldn't see what was so all-fired funny.

The hardest part was lying to Ella. He had to make up some excuse for going to town in such a hurry. He mumbled something about needing a part for the tractor.

"Whyn't you take me with you?" She said this while rubbing her bare foot up and down his thigh. He was seated on the couch, and she was lying on the other end, her back against the arm. She wore shorts, and his hand played at the hem against her inner thigh.

"Just got in a hurry, I guess. You looked awful busy in your garden."

"Phoo, Buck. You know I can hoe in that garden anytime. I don't get to go to town that often. I could have got that lace I want from Murphy's."

"Lace?" He thought to distract her.

"For my baptism dress. You know, I told you. I want some lace on the bottom and around the sleeves."

"You're going to be the most beautiful woman ever baptized in that pond."

"Go on. You know I'm the only woman ever baptized in that pond."

She played at kicking him. He caught her foot, lifted it to his lips, and kissed her toes.

Later, after they'd made love, he said, "Take the truck tomorrow and go on to town. I don't need it."

"Are you sure?"

He smarted at the excitement in her voice. But next day, while she was gone looking for lace for her baptismal gown, he hitched a plow to the tractor, drove it down to the dry gulch, made a trench. By hand, he shoveled in the birds, covered them over with dirt, stomped the mass grave down with his boots.

He argued with himself constantly. If he told Ella about the blackbirds, maybe she'd take it for a sign that the baptism wasn't supposed to happen. Even if she didn't see it as a sign, maybe she'd feel creeped out about having the baptism on the site. But did he want her to be creeped out about their own land? He'd never kept anything from her before. If it wasn't for the stupid baptism, he would have told her, taken her to the dry gulch to see the burial trench. They would have consoled each other. He would have felt safe. He hated the way her being saved made him second-guess everything he'd been sure of before.

Three days later Joe called and reported that the University of Nebraska Extension Service said there have been, over the years, other reports of mass bird deaths. No one knows why. There are lots of theories—disease, power lines, storms—but no real proof of anything. Blackbirds flock together in roosts, sometimes thousands or millions at a time. Apparently, that makes them more vulnerable. Hell, maybe one bird goes bonkers, and the rest just follow. They don't call them birdbrains for nothing. And then Joe laughed and hung up. So, that was that.

Buck decided not to say anything to Ella.

After that, Buck was on edge. Waiting for the sky to fall. Every morning he looked out on the yard with trepidation.

"Are you okay?" Ella asked.

"Sure thing," he lied, trying to lace his voice with optimism.

Meanwhile, Buck had work to do. He drove to Scottsbluff, this time asking Ella if she wanted to come along. She said no, she had sewing to finish up. He went to a landscapers' outfit and bought as much river rock as he thought necessary. More than he could afford. Next day, wearing hip waders, he hauled bucketfuls of rock into the pond, spread it as best he could on the muddy bottom. He had to work hard to pull his feet out of the sucking mire, but by the end of the day, he'd made a neat little platform in the middle of the pond with a path leading to it. The area was smaller than he'd hoped, but as long as Ella and the preacher stayed on the rocks, they'd be fine.

On the Friday before the baptism, he hauled three dried-out logs down by the pond, leveled the ground under them so some of the onlookers could sit. With a scythe he chopped at cattails and marsh grass on the side of the pond where Ella would enter. He tested out the rock lining to make sure it was secure. Finished, he sat on one of the logs and let his eyes sweep over the prairie. Dotted with sunflowers and goldenrod, grass rippling in the breeze, sprinkled with grasshoppers and buzzing insects, it did look like Paradise. A sudden storm could still sweep up and spoil the day, but nothing was forecast. He knew he'd have to sneak out of bed early tomorrow to make sure no more blackbirds fell out of the sky overnight.

The next day dawned bright and sunny. People began to show up about 10:30 a.m., brought casseroles and salads, pies and cakes. The whole thing had the aura of a festival. At 11:00, the crowd paraded down to the pond on Buck's mown path, except for Ella, who stayed behind to dress and make her entry. Buck was careful to show Reverend Kane the path of rocks and the platform under the shallow water.

At 11:15 a.m. Ella came down the path in her white gauzy dress, her blond hair streaming behind. She carried a nosegay of wild roses, looking for all the world like a bride on her way to the altar. Buck stood at the end of the path, close to the pond, and when she drew abreast of him, she reached out, took his hand, and smiled with such luminosity that it took his breath away. She dropped his hand, handed her bouquet to Lily's daughter, and stepped onto the stones leading out to the pastor. Buck had cautioned her to wear old shoes because he worried that the stones would hurt her feet, but she chose to walk barefoot into the water, leaving her white flats on the shore.

Reverend Kane waited for her in the middle of the pond, wearing a white robe over old suit pants, also in bare feet, the water level just above his knees. He stretched his hand out to Ella as she walked forward, drew her in front of him, and faced her sideways to himself. He asked if she willingly sought to join the church through baptism. Ella's voice rang out clearly: "Yes, I do." Then the

Reverend said a short prayer. He braced his right arm behind Ella's back. In his left, he held a white linen cloth that he placed over her nose and mouth. As he laid Ella backward into the water, he said, "Buried with Christ in baptism," and just as he started the next phrase, "Risen to walk . . . ," he lost his balance. Struggling to stay upright, he shifted his right foot off the small platform of rocks. The mud pulled at his right leg, throwing him farther off-balance. Still hanging on to Ella, her weight pitched him forward, and to escape falling on top of her, the good reverend dropped his hold on her and put his hands out to brace his fall. His hands hit the mud, sunk up to his elbows, and for one horrifying but hilarious moment, the minister was stretched over Ella like a croquet hoop while she floated, her white dress spread around her like a water lily. The crowd tried to suppress the giggles, but when Reverend Kane, with the only means available to him, pulled one arm out of the mud and pushed down on Ella's stomach to get enough traction to pull the other arm out, the crowd erupted into laughter.

Buck watched all this in a seething cascade of emotion. Horror— he should have spent more money and bought more rocks. Sympathy—poor Ella, to be made to look so foolish. Amusement— the whole scene so off-kilter, how could you not laugh? And then, bewildered awe—what a stroke of luck! He wouldn't have to say a word. Human nature being what it was, people would yak about this all through the luncheon. Ella would be embarrassed. Why, he could even come to her defense. She'd give it up, this ridiculous quest, and come back to him, relieved that she had escaped. They'd never have to speak of it again, and everything would go back to normal.

He felt vindicated, victorious, and by then, Reverend Kane had retrieved his footing and managed to raise Ella up out of the water, completing the phrase, "Risen to walk in newness of life." Her white dress clung to her body in just the way Buck had feared, her blond hair wet and plastered to her head. She did not falter, but stepped serenely toward the shore where Lily waited with a large towel to drape around her dripping body. Reverend Kane made it to shore, too, without mishap, looking shaken and sheepish, met by his wife, who wrapped him and patted him and murmured reassuring wifely things.

Buck waited, all through the potluck luncheon, for someone to make fun of the minister's folly. To his amazement, no one did. All anyone did was congratulate Ella as if she'd accomplished a tremendous feat, run a marathon or earned a purple ribbon at the fair. As for Ella, she seemed to have no awareness of anything having gone wrong. She basked in their attention, played the part of the gracious hostess.

When everyone finally went home, they had a light supper. They sat on the porch into the evening. Buck watched Ella for signs, sensing that something had changed, though he couldn't say in what way. She thanked him for all he had done to help prepare for the day.

Later in bed, she nested her head against his shoulder, sighed deeply. Buck thought if she were a cat, she would purr. "It was lovely, wasn't it, Buck?"

Buck swallowed. This was his moment. He could burst her bubble, bring her home. But then, he thought of Ella's face as she rose from the water, translucent with joy. He couldn't follow her there, and he knew it. He simply didn't believe. Not like that. He wondered if she knew and what she would do with the knowledge once it came to her. He tightened his grip on her and made a noise low in his throat, not sure what he intended.

"I love you, Buck," she whispered.

He heard her breath deepen. He knew sleep would not come easy and not for a while. He turned his head toward the window and the moonlit sky. Who would believe blackbirds could rain from the sky? Or, for that matter, that Sputnik could rocket into orbit? What else? he wondered. What else is out there, lurking and unexplored in the deepening night?

CONFESSIONS

Rev. Everett Kane carries a load of secrets into Pighetti's Café on a rainy Monday in May. Everett sits in the third booth from the door, his customary spot, and watches the street. The front window offers a fractured view, the top scrawled with PIGHETTI's in black and red script, the bottom draped with lace curtains. Everett watches all the same. He thinks of himself as a watcher, someone who stands by while other people suffer, bleed, get born and die. The best he can do is hold their hands. Pray, of course. He does that.

He takes note of Mr. Lindstrom, sheltered under the awning of Bert's Drugs. The blind man and his dog wait patiently for a single customer who might buy a handmade broom from the bundle leaned up against the storefront. Arnold Summers ambles kitty-cornered across the street, returning to his hardware store from the post office, no doubt hung over from a bender the night before. Mr. Logan's car, a brand-new 1955 Bel Air Chevy, is parked in front of his bank, I LIKE IKE stickered on the rear bumper. Everett knows too much about the people of this town.

"Coffee, Reverend Kane?"

Everett looks up into the bright face of Delores, Pighetti's niece, who isn't young anymore. Case in point. Everett knows Delores went home with Trevor Lang one night a few weeks ago. Trevor's wife, Arlene, comes to the church every time Trevor acts up, even though they're separated.

"Coffee suits me fine, Delores." Her red hair knots behind her ears in a tiny bun. She squints her eyes. Everett sees, as others do, a pig face. He knows he shouldn't think this. For penance, he drinks his coffee black.

Everett rubs his fingers across his forehead. His hair has thinned since his last birthday, when he turned forty-five, and he's not used to feeling his forehead naked under his hand. He removes his glasses, places them on the black tabletop in front of him, and digs at his eyes until color spots kaleidoscope. He watches the rain drizzle across the window, but he can't get away from his thoughts. Mr. Bigelow, the school principal, has a problem with pornography. Lillian Dellman drinks too much, hides the bottles from her husband. A sixteen-year-old girl in his own congregation is afraid of her stepfather. Everett worries that she may be trying to tell him something else, something he's not prepared to hear.

"You okay?" Everett is surprised to see Delores still standing by his table.

"Sure. Fine." You can go to hell for lying. He used to think that. Now, he knows that people need lies. He deals in lies. People tell him devastating truths, and he pretends it doesn't matter. God forgives. God has a plan. It's a weird exchange rate. They cash in their anxieties, and he blots them out. Until the next week or day or hour when the spiritual dust wears off.

Everett smells bacon frying in Pighetti's kitchen. Delores pours a coffee refill, steaming. He catches a glimpse of his reflection in the oil that slicks on the surface, a result of Reach's questionable water supply. The caramel roll squats on his plate, mired in sugary goo.

The brass bell on Pighetti's door clanks. The door is shoved open by Dr. Reuben Silverman. Reuben is one of three doctors in town, but he's the only Jew and the only person with a peg leg. He lost his left leg during the war. He says he likes wearing the peg because it reminds him of members of his family who disappeared during the Holocaust. They suffered so much more than this, he says. I should complain?

Dr. Silverman slides in the booth opposite Reverend Kane. An unlikely pair, the Baptist minister and a Jewish doctor, in a small town in Nebraska. Reuben takes off his black jacket, holds it at arm's length in the aisle, shakes off the raindrops, then tosses it into the corner of the booth. The red plastic upholstery sucks at the back of his damp pant legs. He's older than Everett in years, but also in experience.

Reuben lifts a finger and nods to Delores. She smiles as most people do when they see the doctor. He's their resident foreigner. He's so far out of the fray of Catholic-Protestant mistrust that his oddities don't register on the local scale. He does his job, keeps to himself, and Reverend Kane likes him. Good enough, for most.

"So?" The doctor turns his attention to Everett. "How's your soul today?"

Everett looks up with sad eyes. "It's raining."

"Ah." Reuben turns in the booth and looks toward the street. Odd, Everett thinks, how people will look back to verify where they've been. Like returning to the scene of a crime. Or bringing up old, painful topics.

Delores sets a scalding cup of coffee in front of Reuben. She retreats and sits on a counter stool, absorbed in *Look* magazine. They are the only customers.

The two men sit for a time in silence, a habit of theirs. Everett notices Reuben holds his hand to his mouth and breathes against his fingers. A shiver passes through the doctor's arm and over his body.

"And you?" It's easy for Everett to ask Reuben. Even if Reuben tells him *things*, Reuben won't expect an answer. Reuben doesn't buy Everett's God. Reuben thinks Jesus Christ is too young to understand the age-old ills of the universe. They've been over this ground before, and to Everett's great relief Reuben has refused to be either insulted or converted.

Reuben gathers himself before he speaks. Everett watches the effort, the squaring of the shoulders, the deep intake of breath, the hand pressed firmly against the lips.

"I've come from the Cantwells," Reuben says. Something about the tone, the way he shakes his head.

"Is something wrong?" Everett asks.

"Are they one of your families?"

"Yes. Well, Iris and the kids. We haven't seen Pete in some time. I don't know. People fall away."

Everett lifts his hand, heavy off the table, and lets it drop. He should have gone out there. Anyone can see the Cantwells are a family in trouble. Something's wrong with Pete, the way his feet shuffle. It's a bad time for Iris to be pregnant.

"She has a history of miscarriages," Reuben says.

"Oh? I didn't know that." Everett is genuinely surprised. He could have figured it out, he thinks. Jim must be, what, thirteen? Annie, maybe six. A lot of years between kids.

"The baby—" Reuben lifts his coffee, holds it to his lips, but does not drink.

"It's not time, is it?" Everett knows that he loses track of time. It stretches out endlessly before him, like a dark room he does not want to enter. Yet, at the end of a day, it seems that he has never done the things he meant to do.

Reuben's hands are trembling. His right hand is fixed to the cup, held as if by electric shock. Coffee sloshes over the table. Everett gently lays his palm on Reuben's shaking arm. He steadies the hand until the cup comes to rest on the tabletop. Reuben lifts himself on one haunch, withdraws a wadded handkerchief from his right rear pocket, blows his nose, and stuffs the handkerchief back in place.

"Sorry," Reuben mutters.

"What is it?" Everett asks. He hears the tone of his own voice, the soothing undercurrent. Alarming, how easily he slips into this role.

"The baby came early," Reuben says. "Pete went up to the neighbor's to call me. They don't have a phone."

"Pete's a private man. He must have been scared plenty." Everett pictures Pete Cantwell standing in his overalls outside the door of his nearest neighbor, most certainly his landlord.

"Pete asked me to come out." Reuben's voice sounds strangely flat. Everett picks up on these nuances. "He said Iris wasn't doing so good. He didn't think it was the baby. So, I drove out there last night. Seven miles, sliding around on those country roads. Iris was lying down in the bedroom. There's a crib crammed in the corner. Annie still sleeps there. They don't have water in the house. Just a washstand in the kitchen with a bucket and a dipper."

Reuben pauses to take a drink from his cup. The rain outside gushes in waves, whole buckets dumped down the front of Pighetti's window. Everett remembers a car wash he saw in Omaha, newfangled with brushes and water squashing at the window like this. He worries about water rising in the river. He pictures basements full of water, people canoeing down Main Street, the street dumping into the North Platte River, then the Platte, the mighty Mississippi, down into the Gulf. If enough rain falls, he can step into a canoe and not get out until he's crossed into another country.

"Everett." Reuben's voice scrapes at his name, throwing it up from the bottom of a barrel. "What do you think of playing God?"

Everett is unprepared for Reuben's question, even though it has been on his mind for years.

"No one plays God, Reuben. No one would want the responsibility."

"Suppose God is not around?"

Everett squirms in his seat. "Reuben, don't talk to me like this. Because if you want proof of spirit, I can't give it to you."

Reuben leans forward in his seat. His voice rasps. "I'm asking what we are supposed to do when God is absent?"

"I don't know. I don't know what we are supposed to do. I'm not allowed to think God is absent, by the way. I'm only allowed to think God has other things in mind."

"Other things?"

"Bigger things."

"Yes, yes. But what do we do in the meantime while God is working on bigger things. Heh?"

"Stand it. That's what we are supposed to do. Stand it until something better comes along."

"Suppose you have to make a decision? Suppose you can't stand by because you are the one who must decide?"

Everett starts to feel flattened, like a tire losing air. He sneaks a sideways look at Delores and is relieved to see that she's absorbed in her magazine. "Don't ask me this, don't . . ." Everett bats the air with the back of his hand. Then, he leans across the table and lowers his voice. "Reuben. What do you want?"

"Peace, Everett." Reuben's voice is calm. His doctor voice, Everett thinks. Handling him with velvet. "To be able to sleep at night. What do you want?"

Everett tugs at the gluey mess of his caramel roll. His breath comes fast and hard. He's got to start getting more exercise. Give up these caramel rolls. He needs some air.

"Nothing," Everett says at last. "I want nothing."

To Everett's surprise, Reuben laughs. "That's a good way to get it," Reuben says.

"Get what?"

"Nothing. You want nothing, you get nothing. A good plan. Wish I'd thought of it."

Everett knows he's being laughed at. He doesn't care. Laughing is better than all this probing. He chuckles along with Reuben.

"Can I tell you something?" Reuben asks.

"Please don't." Everett smiles, but he means it.

"I've never told anyone here."

Everett shifts in his seat. "Some things are better off left alone." He knows that once Reuben tells him, things won't be the same. People hand over their secrets, little bits of themselves for his safekeeping, and then they walk away. Everett doesn't want to lose his only friend.

Reuben sweeps aside Everett's objections, if he hears them at all. His voice opens. "In Warsaw, they herded us into a ghetto. You know about that?"

Everett nods.

"There was so little food. So little of everything. People were being shipped out every day. We heard rumors about camps, death camps. People were dying. It was a matter of when, not if."

Reuben stops. Everett waits and watches the rain. An absurd Bible verse flutters through his mind. *Wash me, and I shall be whiter than snow.*

Reuben begins again, falteringly. "In Warsaw, everything turned upside down. I stole bread and medicine from the mouths of the sick. I doomed the old, and sometimes"—here Reuben's voice drops to a whisper—"the very young."

"What could you do? You had no choice." Everett remembers the first half of the verse. *Purge me with hyssop, and I shall be clean.* What, Everett wonders, is hyssop?

"You completely miss the point, Everett. I had to choose. Poor old Mrs. Keynes, who once handed me candy sticks over her grocery counter, or Joseph Berger, a miserable man keeping twenty others alive with connections to the black market. Which deserves to live? Tell me, Everett, what would you have done?"

"You did everything you could." Everett offers this, hoping that Reuben will take it and shut up.

"No." Reuben reaches out a hand and grasps Everett's wrist. "Not everything. I saved myself."

Everett doesn't know what to do or say. Odd. Without his catalogue of condolences, he isn't sure what is required of him. His mind is sloshing around somewhere in the Bible, over snatches of old hymns—*showers of blessing*—while his eyes watch Reuben's face. Reuben's gray hair sticks up in peaks ringed about his balding head. He looks strangely like a baby chick, vulnerable and naked in the world.

"It was a girl," Reuben says.

Everett's mind lurches back to the Cantwell baby.

"She was too early. Pain, and I had nothing to give her. At the most, she would have had a few hours of suffering."

"Poor Iris." Everett is relieved. An early death. Not so bad. A baby who could not live. One gets over these things.

"I put my hand over her mouth." The flat voice again, as uninflected as miles of prairie.

"You mean, she died. She died, and then you covered her."

"I put my hand over her mouth." Reuben stares straight at him.

Everett registers shock. This is it, then. He wants to run. He actually shuffles his feet under the table. He whips his head from side to side, where, where can he go? What kind of world is this? God, Everett thinks, you bungle everything. You had no right to use him like that. He feels Reuben's steady gaze on him and forces himself to look at Reuben's face. He follows the pain in Reuben's eyes to the hollows of his cheeks, to his clenched jaw, and his own breathing slows as he focuses on his friend, as good a man as he has ever known.

Everett lays his hand gently on Reuben's arm. "God wasn't absent, Reuben. You were there."

Reuben's face crumples, and he looks away. No more words come to Everett. There is nothing to do but sit with Reuben in silence.

The two men part outside Pighetti's. Reuben claps Everett on the back and hauls off to his black Chevy. Everett lingers on the sidewalk, looking up and down the street. There's Mr. Summers, rolling out the awnings over the hardware store windows. Children are shrieking and stomping in gutter puddles left after the rain. Everett offers his arm to old Mrs. Watson as she walks her well-trained Pekinese to the beauty parlor. On the way, Everett reaches down, places his hand within the hand of the blind man sitting patiently under the awning of Bert's Drugs, and exchanges four shiny quarters for a broom.

LESSONS AT THE PO

On the day of the murder, Elsie Morton goes about her business slipping envelopes into the brass boxes of the Bluestem Post Office. George Washington looks up at her, unsmiling, from purple three-cent stamps. Finished with her job, she lumbers to the kitchen in her cramped apartment behind the PO, lowers herself into a chair, and pours a glass of iced tea. A peeled edge of torn upholstery gouges her thigh where her short muumuu has hiked up. She lifts one leg, the plastic seat tearing from her sticky body with a sickening suck-suck. She sets the leg down again, sighs, and mops at her neck with a balled-up hankie.

Beyond her kitchen window, the neighbor kids loll on the front porch of their abandoned storefront home. They go to school across the North Platte River, in Reach, but now it's summer and too hot to swivel a Hula-Hoop, too hot to do anything but lie in the shade and hallucinate. As if the heat weren't bad enough, there's this killer wind. The air hums with static. Tumbleweeds pitch across open fields, and whirlwinds steal the topsoil. Whine and grit have settled in Elsie's ears, rented rooms inside her head.

Elsie and her husband, Banjo, don't have a fan in this place. No wall-to-wall carpet. No picture window. No decent overhead light. There's a couch, a black-and-white TV, this kitchen table. On her right, a sink and refrigerator. Behind her, a two-burner stove. The room is littered with sheet music, scraps of fabric, whiffs of feather, dirty dishes in the sink, spilled corn flakes on the floor. Perched on a footstool, a pair of silver high-heeled shoes, open-toed and sling-backed. They belong to Cindy Lou, who moved across the river last weekend to live with Wade Schumacher in sin, without the benefit of marriage. Elsie tried to talk her out of it by reciting a litany of women done wrong, starting with Elsie's own mother, whose husband ran off with a tattooed girl from a traveling circus. Cindy Lou said anything was better than living in this place. Pigsty, is what she called it. She packed her clothes, her graduation picture from Reach High, the buffalo salt and pepper shakers from their one family trip to the Black Hills, and a heap of brush rollers in cardboard boxes, and carried it all out to Wade's pickup. He waited for her with the engine running. After all that, she forgot her prom shoes. Those silver slippers.

Elsie hefts herself out of the chair and caroms her way from the table to the sink, to the stove, through the too narrow doorway into a back bedroom. She rummages through paper sacks and digs around under shoe boxes looking for a piano piece called *Tarantella*.

When the bell rings, she trudges back to the front half of the apartment. The door's wide open in an effort to catch a breeze from the lobby of the PO. Not wanting to take more steps, Elsie waves in her piano student, nine-year-old Annie Cantwell.

"Whew," Elsie says, fanning herself with her hand. "Hot enough for you?"

Annie shrugs. She's a skinny kid, stands there with her books clasped in front of her. Lank brown hair, watchful eyes, crooked teeth hiding behind a closed mouth.

"Sit on down a minute." Elsie motions at the table, but Annie moves toward the orange flowered couch. She pushes aside an ashtray mounded with paper clips, lays her music down on the corner of a blond end table, crushing further a frilly crocheted doily that needs starch and ironing. She picks up a pile of clean laundry from the sofa, holds it, and turns corners for a while, searching for a place to unload it. Finally she sits with socks and shirts cradled in her lap. Elsie watches all this with something like awe, the prissiness of it, and then, the girl's discomfort.

Elsie oozes into her kitchen chair and lifts her glass of tea. "It's the wind that gets to me," she says. "Drives me straight out of my mind."

"My mom'll be back in half an hour," Annie says.

"Right." Elsie sets her glass down. Using her arms to rise from the chair, she hangs on to the edge of the table, dizzy, heat piled up on her like wool blankets she can't throw off. "Well, then, we best get started."

Before Annie can budge, Banjo's pickup pulls up outside. He slams the door, lunges across the lobby, and bangs into the room. For a tall, bony man, he takes up a lot of space. His face and body are hard and dried out, like beef jerky. He wears cowboy clothes: checkered yoked shirt, boots, and peeled-on jeans. He crosses to the sink, runs the water hard, and washes his hands over piles of dirty dishes, splashing water onto the linoleum. His voice barks across his shoulder. "Got my supper on?"

"Banjo?" Elsie leans into the table. "It's four thirty. What are you doing home this time of day?"

"I ain't coming home later, that's for sure. Open me a can of beans."

Banjo's voice sounds like gravel under truck tires, raw and punched. He puts one hand on the back of a yellow chair piled with boxes of soda crackers and Wheaties and tips the chair so the boxes fall and scatter across the floor, collide with the cat dish, ricochet off shoes and magazines. Then he turns the chair backward and straddles the seat. He spreads open *Field and Stream* on the table, paying no attention to the pitcher of iced tea, dirty glasses, piles of unread newspapers, leftover breakfast dishes, or silverware that has strayed from its drawer.

"Watch out. You'll break something," Elsie warns.

Banjo grunts but keeps right on reading. He picks his teeth with a toothpick. His right leg bounces up and down, and he glances from his magazine to the door. Elsie moves over to the cupboard above the sink. She wipes the top of a can of pork and beans with the tail of her skirt while she searches through a drawer for a can opener.

"Thought you was goin' hunting with Floyd today."

"Did," Banjo says. He stretches out his hand for the can of beans. Elsie sets it in his palm. He picks up a spoon from the ones scrambled on the table and feeds himself from the can. Elsie stands behind him, hands shelved on mountainous hips.

Banjo keeps on shoveling beans. Elsie watches him, too tired to move. Out of the corner of her eye, she sees Annie shift on the couch and push the footstool with her toe. The silver high heels teeter until one shoe clatters to the floor. Banjo's head jerks up.

"Annie's here for her lesson," Elsie says.

Banjo turns his head and looks at Annie. He works his tongue in his cheek. "Shut the door," he says, diving back into his beans.

Elsie's piano is wedged in a tiny room off the living area of their apartment. With the door shut, it feels like a closet and smells like old work boots, but on this Tuesday, Elsie closes the door and leaves Banjo on the other side, picking his teeth and spooning beans from a can. Elsie moves her bulk around, shifts piles of sheet music from the piano bench to the floor, throws a red corduroy jacket off a broke-down chair. After a few minutes, there's a cleared space for Annie to sit down.

Annie opens the music to *Lady of Spain*. She romps through the first line, pounds hard and fast, her breath quickening, and Elsie imagines ruffled skirts and heaving bosoms and a man's penetrating gaze while a familiar shiver of alarm runs up her spine. What's to become of this girl? She needs music like other people need air. She'll have to learn to bridle that passion, the way women do, before it propels her into danger, before she launches a revolution from which she can't return. She should stop giving this girl Latin pieces. Why, for God's sake, was she looking for *Tarantella*? Learn to play *pianissimo*, she should say. But she closes her eyes and rides on the tumultuous waves, through the second chorus and to the end of *I adore you* before somebody pounds on the piano room door.

"Elsie, you in there?"

"Now, who in blazes is that?" Elsie mutters under her breath. She heaves herself out of the rickety chair and opens the door. Sheriff Pinski stands with his hands on his hips, brown uniform, sweat rings large under his arms.

"Bob? What are you doing here?"

"Best you come on out here." The sheriff nods his head at Annie. "You, too, Annie. Best you call your parents. Tell them to come and get you early."

"Now hold on there, Bob." Elsie hasn't been paid yet. What's the matter with everybody? "Her folks don't have a phone." With one hand, Elsie motions Annie back to her seat on the piano bench.

Bob speaks softly to Elsie. "Well. I expect this is going to be all over town anyway." The sheriff picks at the plastic liner on his shirt pocket. He studies his shoelaces. Elsie worries about Sheriff Bob because his daddy and his granddaddy both shot themselves, and who knows but maybe those things run in families. He seems nervous now, and Elsie's glad he doesn't have his finger on the trigger of a gun. "I got to take Banjo here in for a few questions. That's all there is to it."

"Questions," Elsie repeats. "What for?"

Banjo shifts in his seat like he's plunked down on a cocklebur. "What's going on?" Banjo asks.

"We found Floyd Markham's body down by the river." The sheriff gazes over their heads, trying to find some place to put his eyes that offers a more restful picture.

"He'd been shot." The sheriff takes his fingers off the plastic pouch and rubs them on the front of his shirt. "He's dead."

"Can't be." Banjo stands up and looks Sheriff Pinski straight in the eye. "I was just with him a few hours ago. We was hunting down there on the old Jenkins place."

"Well." The sheriff's hand roams along the line of his jaw. "That's right where we found him, Banjo. It don't look good, what with, and all."

"What do you mean, what with?" Elsie asks, as if she hasn't heard the gossip about Banjo and Floyd's wife, Betty. Floyd is Banjo's best friend. And what does Betty see in Banjo that'd make her give up a secure life with the county surveyor?

"Well now, Elsie." The sheriff sounds like a man who resents having to do his job and resents her for making him do it. "I think you know what I mean."

Then, in a real quiet voice, Banjo says, "I been home most the afternoon. What time'd you say you found the body?"

"That true?" the sheriff asks Elsie. "Has Banjo been home most the afternoon?"

Banjo runs his fingers through his hair, sweeps back the few long strands that have slipped out of the rubber band at the base of his neck. Then he speaks straight into his can of beans. "You know, Honey. I told you straight off how Floyd and I packed it in early."

Elsie's jaw hangs slack, her face stuck a few minutes behind in the conversation. The sheriff turns all his attention on Elsie. "Floyd was shot at real close range. Not that long ago, from the looks of it. Right in the side of the head, like he didn't suspect a thing."

Elsie steps aside, to weigh things in her mind. Banjo's no picnic, God knows. He can be downright mean. Half the time, he can't hold a job. Still, they've been together twenty-six years, hell, they grew up together. What would it do to Cindy Lou, her dad in jail? And who else would want a woman like her? She's not thinking about Floyd and his blown-away head. She can't think about that now.

"'Course he was here, Bob." She whispers it, more or less, trying it out on her tongue. "Banjo, here, he came home and said they'd had enough today. Too damn hot, and the wind nearly bowled them over. You know what this whole summer's been like. Would you want to be out there in the heat of the day?"

She lets her voice get strong, there at the last. She makes it sound like Reverend Kane when he's working himself up for a big finish, laying off the fire and not a single drop of water for all us sinners and heading over into glory if you will take the name of Jesus. Elsie has the name of Jesus singing in her voice, and there's not a thing Sheriff Bob can do about it.

Except. She forgot about Annie.

Sheriff Bob takes a few steps toward Annie. He kneels down in front of the piano bench. "Annie," Sheriff Bob says in a no-nonsense voice. "Did you see Banjo when you came in for your lesson this afternoon?"

Elsie watches Annie squirm on the bench. This little Miss Priss, straight A's, perfect do-right-fuss-budget kid is going to tell on her, send Banjo to the pen, maybe get her arrested for obstructing justice. But Annie says nothing. She sits in stony silence, like she's none too bright and didn't understand the question.

"Did you see Banjo, Annie?"

Annie bites her lip. When she removes her teeth, tiny red beads appear. Elsie risks a sidewise look at Banjo. He's trying to hide it, but she reads the smirk on his face.

When Elsie turns back, Annie is looking at her over Sheriff Bob's head. Slowly, Elsie realizes that Annie is waiting for a signal. The kid would lie for her, if she tells her to. For her. All Elsie needs to do is nod her head, and Banjo will walk free.

Elsie closes her eyes. She'd snort if she knew how. She'd bay at the moon, bugle like a randy elk. She'd wail like an Irishwoman at a wake. Laugh like a crazy relative hidden in the attic. Instead, she puts her hand on Sheriff Bob's shoulder.

"Leave her alone," she says.

"I'm just asking . . . ," the sheriff says.

"He wasn't here." It's not hard to tell the truth. In fact, it falls out of her mouth. She says it again. "He wasn't here."

"Annie?" The sheriff's voice is gentle, but solid like a cellar door.

"No," Annie whispers.

"He wasn't here?" the sheriff asks.

Annie shakes her head. "He came later," she breathes.

As soon as the sheriff hustles Banjo out the door, Elsie sits herself down at the table. She rustles up a half-eaten package of chocolate chip cookies and stuffs two in her mouth. She takes a couple swigs of the tea warming in her glass. Annie stands in the doorway of the piano room, watching her.

Elsie waves a hand in the air. "Ohmygod," she says. "Ohmygod, mygod, ohmygod." Elsie's voice breaks, and she closes her mouth, sniffs hard through her nose. She looks away, out her kitchen window. When she turns again, Annie has seated herself at the table.

"You think he's guilty." Annie states it. Not a question.

Elsie stares at her. She's covered for Banjo so many times, she never stopped to think that he might not have done what he was accused of.

"I don't know what I think. Man like Banjo . . ." Elsie's voice drifts away.

"Yeah?"

"Sometimes he wakes up in the morning, swings his feet out of bed, and lands on the wrong side of luck."

"What do you mean?"

Elsie looks at Annie's puckered face. She's never going to be pretty, too much forehead, the chin too small. Maybe life will be kind to her, likely it won't. Elsie manages a crooked smile.

"You want a cookie?"

Annie shakes her head. Elsie helps herself to two more. Once again, she turns toward the window. While she is looking out onto nothing, she hears Annie creep back to the piano bench. She's ripping through *Lady of Spain*, the notes banging against the cords of Elsie's tight chest. Elsie wipes her wet face with the back of her hand. To no one but herself, she speaks. "Play it loud, kid. Play it free."

AFTER DEATH

Hazel Mueller makes her rounds at the Reach hospital. She pushes a cart with ammonia, disinfectant, paper towels, window cleaner, dust spray, abrasive powder, a broom, feather duster, mop, and bucket. Some of the rooms are carpeted. These she has to come back to with the vacuum cleaner. She lugs the beast down the hall, cursing the stupidity of whoever designed this place. Flat roof that leaks. Carpet that carries infection. The old hospital has been turned into county offices, or she might raise a petition to move back there. It had only ten rooms, and they were small.

Still, it's not a bad job. Cleaning up the dirt of other people's lives. Sweeping up behind them. Swabbing their shit out of bathroom stools. Scrubbing vomit off the floor. Smelling the decay of sickness. Tossing out bloody tissues, caked gauze, drooping plants. It's not so bad, sanitizing a room after death. Wiping the slate clean.

Hazel enters room 5. She's timed it so the patient is out of the room, down the hall doing physical therapy. Hazel hates talking. She hates small talk and conversation. President Reagan is smiling all over the TV tube; she turns him off. She runs her fingers over the window ledge and decides not to bother dusting it. She's lasted at this job twelve years, first at the old hospital, now this one, because she's learned how to pace herself.

This is Nellie Watkins's room. Broke her leg. Fell down on her porch and had to wait for hours until Judy Cochero came to pick her up for pinochle. That can happen to you when you live alone in a small town. Hazel knows this for a fact.

She sits down on the edge of Nellie's bed. She runs her hands over the pillow cover, smooths it, and picks up the cards propped on Nellie's bed stand. Any of them that say *God bless you* or *I've been praying for you* don't interest her. She knows better, ever since Ralph left her for that Norcroft woman. There's one card, though. It's white with white raised roses on it and *Thinking of you* across the top. The sender has written a special note inside. *I think of you every day, with love.* Hazel runs her fingers over those two words, *with love.* Then, she pockets the card, hitches herself to her feet, and goes about her cleaning.

Later, when she gets home, she stands the card up on her night-stand. She takes down the one from last week, the one with pink roses and *thoughts of you.* The one that Mabel Becker's husband sent. He wrote, in his own hand, *I don't think I can live without you.* Mabel went home, but she has cancer and the chemotherapy isn't working. Still, every night for a week, Hazel read that card before going to sleep.

The next week Mabel Becker is back in the hospital, and something else bad happens. Hazel gets paired up with Iris Cantwell. She's supposed to show Iris the routine. She's supposed to take Iris with her room to room and put up with Iris's constant chatter. Iris knows every patient, too, and takes it on herself to cheer them up. She thinks she's an expert on coping because her husband died some years back from Huntington's disease.

"Nellie, how're you doing today?" That's Iris. Hazel humps over her mop in the bathroom.

"Not too bad." Nellie's voice ripples like water when you throw a stone.

Hazel peeks around the corner of the bathroom and sees Iris fluttering around the room, working while she talks. Iris sprays window cleaner on the windows.

"My goodness." Iris again. She never shuts up. "These windows are a fright. Doesn't anybody ever wash them on the outside?"

Later, when they're sitting in the staff room over a cup of coffee, the nurses sucking on cigarettes, Iris brings up those windows. Hazel never sits at the table. She parks in a chair by the wall reading a book. Iris laughs with Barbara and Lucille.

"Mabel's back." Lucille says this. She's got short brown hair, full lips. She's been called perky. Hazel hates perky.

"I don't think she'll go home this time." Barbara Harris, red-haired and aging.

"I've got to go and see her," Iris chimes in. "Mabel was one of my hostesses years ago. She used to have two or three parties every year. We had so much fun. Once we walked down to the North Platte River and went fishing. We didn't catch anything, but when we got back, Barney had a fish fry going for all of us. Catfish he'd caught the day before." Iris's hands fly while she tells this story about her life as a Tupperware dealer. Barbara and Lucille eat it up. Iris must be past sixty. She dyes her hair, anyone can see that.

That afternoon, Hazel putters around the operating room while Iris fills buckets of sudsy water and carries them outside. Using a long-handled mop, she scrubs the windows. Then, Iris climbs on a stepladder and rubs each pane dry with a cloth. She goes around the entire hospital while Hazel vacuums the carpeted visitors' lounge and the five carpeted rooms.

When Iris is outside Mabel Becker's room, Hazel can see her from the lounge. Iris paints a smiley face on the glass with her mop and suds, then knocks on the window and waves at Mabel. Mabel raises herself up on a thin arm. She makes a shooing motion at Iris and laughs.

Hazel moves slowly behind the heavy vacuum cleaner. She sweeps it back and forth, monotonous motion, the roar wrapped around her like a cocoon.

Iris is a regular Mrs. Clean. She insists on corners and cobwebs that Hazel has ignored for years. She drags her cheerfulness around the hospital like a pet on a leash. Lucille and Barbara and Jerry, the hospital administrator, act like she's God's gift. Hazel has been doing the dirty work for twelve years without so much as a thank-you, and now they fall over each other dumping praise on Iris. Barbara brings oatmeal cookies with raisins for the coffee room. Nellie Watkins goes home earlier than expected, and Iris gets credit for it. Hazel finds it harder and harder to get out of bed in the morning.

Mabel Becker's condition grows worse. She's entering that phase when cancer patients turn on those they love. They shut the door on them. Hazel remembers how her mother did that. Couldn't stand the sight of her. Mabel's husband still sits with her every day, but even he can't take too much of it. Iris chats him up, too. She explains how Mabel isn't turning her back on *him*, it's the cancer.

Later, Reverend Fowler stops Iris in the hall. Hazel flips a feather duster over the framed posters hanging in the hallway, insipid pictures of children and angels and kittens. She's at least two rooms away from the pastor and Iris, but she hears everything. They take no notice of her. She might as well be a potted plant.

"Some of us are coming to lay hands on Mabel, Iris. We hope you'll join us." Reverend Fowler, a weasel-faced man, speaks in a grating nasal voice. He's decent, everybody says, but no one can stand to listen to him preach for long. He knows it, though, and keeps his morning messages mercifully short.

Iris leans on the handle of her dust mop. Her head wags up and down, a signal that she's giving the pastor's request serious thought. "Reverend Fowler, do you mean to pray for a cure?"

"Of course. God can heal anything, if we only ask."

"Mabel's dying, Pastor. She's dying of cancer."

Hazel moves toward Iris and the pastor. She's already dusted the frames going that direction, but no one knows that.

"Nothing is too big for God, Iris."

Iris chews on her lip for a moment. She lifts her chin. "No, Pastor. I can't do that. I can't go and lay hands on Mabel and ask God to make her well. But I will go and see her on my own. I will do that."

Hazel sees that the pastor is none too pleased. A smirk grows at the corners of her mouth. So, finally, someone else has run headlong into Iris's stubbornness. Iris of the last word. Iris who knows the right thing to do. Iris, the caller of shots. Iris, Iris, Iris. It's enough to make Hazel puke.

Hazel moves through the rest of the day thinking about Iris. Hazel never would have figured her for the cynical type. She could see Iris leading the march on poor Mabel Becker. Cheer up, Mabel, make us all feel better. Thank the Lord, Mabel. God, heal Mabel, amen, amen. Hazel hears the echo of dirt falling on her mother's coffin. After her mother's death, she smelled guilt seeping from her armpits, her groin, the bottoms of her feet. She prayed and prayed, thinking her lack of faith had killed her mother, until that Norcroft woman. After that, she gave up on God and learned how to take care of herself.

Later, in the afternoon, Mabel Becker's husband rushes into the coffee room. He bursts through the door where patients aren't supposed to be, his face red and scared.

"Somebody help me. I don't know what to do with Mabel. She's all upset and crying."

Lucille and Barbara stub out their cigarettes, reach for stethoscopes, and smooth their white shifts over their hips.

"It's the preacher. He says he's going to lay hands on Mabel, and she's fit to be tied over it."

Lucille and Barbara stop, frozen like comic book characters. Hazel watches all of this from her perch in the corner.

"Iris, maybe that's your department," Lucille suggests with a raise of her eyebrows.

"He's your pastor, isn't he?" Barbara says. She's practically panting, she wants out of this so bad.

Before Iris can get to her feet, Hazel shoves herself up, grabs a broom, and moves down the hall to the empty room across from Mabel Becker's. She busies herself in the doorway, jabs at corners with the broom. From here, she can see everything.

"What's the matter, Mabel?" Iris walks right over to the bed. She takes Mabel's withered hand in hers and wipes her eyes with a tissue.

"I don't want them coming here. I don't want them praying over me." Mabel gets this out in fits and starts, hiccuping and blowing her nose. She's got tubes here and there.

Iris glances at Mabel's husband, the one who said he couldn't live without her. Now, he shrugs his shoulders and shakes his head like he's dealing with a two-year-old having a tantrum. He backs away, one step behind the other, until he gets to the doorway, where he bolts. He mutters something about going downtown to Baxter's for a beer. Hazel watches him lurch down the hall. He stops twice and leans against the hallway, but he keeps on walking out the door.

Mabel has calmed down. "I'm not getting well, Iris."

"I know," Iris says matter-of-factly. She could be talking about the weather.

"Nobody will talk to me about it. They all want to pretend it's not happening." Mabel's voice is so weak, Hazel can hardly make out what she's saying.

"They're afraid, is all," Iris says. Hazel almost snorts.

"I suppose they are." Mabel's voice has fallen. Hazel moves forward a step or two. "They're not the ones dying, though." Mabel and Iris chuckle a little. Iris pats Mabel's hand and pulls a chair close to the bed.

"Do you believe in heaven?" Mabel asks.

Iris nods. "I was raised on it," she says. "Mama died when I was young. Daddy not much later. Now, Pete's in heaven, too. I wonder sometimes what it will be like."

"My sister's gone. I lost a baby once. Died with whooping cough."

Mabel rests, quiet for a while. Hazel thinks maybe she has fallen asleep when she opens her eyes. "Thank you, Iris."

Iris starts to stand up. Mabel needs her rest, but she has one more thing on her mind. "Tell the preacher not to come."

Iris stands by Mabel's bed. "Mabel, people love you and don't know how else to show it. Why don't you let them come? What can it hurt?"

Mabel smiles a little, then nods. As Iris moves away, Mabel shoots out a hand and grabs her arm. "Barney . . . What will become of Barney?"

Iris covers Mabel's hand with her own. "Barney will manage, Mabel. But he'll miss you."

That night, Hazel moves restlessly around the living room of her home. She picks up a magazine and lays it down. Once she trudges to the kitchen, slices a piece of chocolate cake, and pours herself a glass of milk. She turns the TV on and off. Finally, she gets herself ready for bed.

In the bathroom she looks at her heavy face in the mirror. Glasses, brown hair. Her eyes dark and saggy underneath. Never was a looker, no sir.

She puts on her striped pajama shirt and drawstring bottoms. Sitting on the edge of the bed, she picks up the card from Mabel's husband. Her feet flop up and down in her slippers, beat a pattern on the carpeted floor. She flings her glasses onto the bed and digs at her eyes with her hand. Then, she rubs the back of her neck. She wishes she had soaked her feet, all day on them and her new shoes chafe.

Glasses in place, still restless, she pulls open the top drawer of her nightstand. She takes out a small stack of photographs and clippings. The top photo shows a mom and dad and a boy about twelve. He's the kid died last year from a rattlesnake bite. Freak accident, out riding by himself, got down to open a fence. The horse returned to the ranch, but by the time they found the kid, he was too far gone. The next is a clipping, obituary for a woman who had a stroke. Another photo, this one of a husband, wife, and a newborn who lived only six days. Hazel works partway through the stack, recalling each room, each diagnosis, until she grows impatient and throws the whole lot on the bed. She reaches again farther back in the drawer and closes her hand around the beads of her mother's rosary. She lifts it from the drawer and holds it across both palms. She feels no heat, even though she knows her mother fingered the black beads every day. She drapes the rosary over the lampshade, stuffs the clippings and photos back into the drawer, climbs into her bed. As she reaches to turn out the light, she turns the dangling crucifix to the back of the lampshade. The last thing she wants to see is a mangled body on a cross.

The next day, Reverend Fowler shows up with his little band. They stand around Mabel's bed, lay hands on her, and ask God to heal her. Barney stands by her head, both hands cradling Mabel's face. Mabel bucks up for their performance, smiles and thanks them.

Three days later, Mabel dies. Iris and Hazel are cleaning out her room, sanitizing it for the next patient.

"Cancer is a hard way to go," Iris says.

Hazel does not respond.

"She's better off, poor soul. I always say I don't fear death, but I don't look forward to the dying."

"Why don't you shut up?"

Hazel turns from her mopping. She feels herself growing large, but she can't help it. Iris looks confused, unfocused. Hazel hardly blames her, the shock, the giant has spoken.

"I can't stand your constant chatter. You never leave alone a single second of silence."

"I'm sorry." Iris turns red, stammering. Hazel thinks she ought to be enjoying this more than she is.

"You don't live in reality, you know that? All your yammering about heaven. You think people are just stacked up over there, like airplanes on a runway?"

Hazel pauses, surprised to discover she wants to know what Iris thinks. Where is my mother, she wants to ask. She waits, but Iris says nothing.

"Well?" she prods.

"What I believe is my business."

"You make it everybody else's business."

"What's that supposed to mean?"

Hazel sees how it is, then. Iris won't tell her. Not her.

"I'm sick to death of your smiling face," Hazel says. Her eyes sting. She needs to get out of here, and fast. Turning, she throws one more line over her shoulder. "I got along fine before you came."

"That's not what I heard."

Hazel stops still. She draws in a ragged breath. She grinds her teeth and hardens her face before she turns to face Iris.

"So, that's what Barbara and Lucille said?"

"It's all over town. No one can stand to work with you. You drive everybody away."

Hazel clings to the handle of her mop. She's afraid if she lets go, she'll fall down.

"You don't care about anyone but yourself," Iris says, her voice trembling and high. She's flailing a feather duster when Jerry rushes in.

Younger than either of them, up to here with administrative hassle, Jerry all but shouts at them. "What the hell is going on in here? We have patients in this hospital who expect a little peace and quiet."

"I can't work with her," Hazel says.

"Fine." Jerry's hands land on his hips. "Then quit."

Hazel turns her back on him. She blinks hard and stares at the blank white wall. She tries to think what else she might do, but comes up with nothing. This job is all she has. She's never had to quit before. The others have always quit.

She turns around slowly. Jerry and Iris are talking softly. She doesn't need to hear the words to know that he's taking Iris's side.

"How about if we divide up the work?" Hazel makes this offer. She might as well be throwing every nickel she owns into a poker pot. "Maybe different shifts? I just don't want to be in the same room with her."

Jerry studies the floor for a minute. He scratches at his head. Then, he turns to Iris.

"That all right with you, Iris?"

"Fine." Iris sets her lips in a prim line. Hazel studies her. She's not going to back down, and Hazel likes that.

"All right." Jerry lets exasperation show in his voice. "I'll see what kind of schedule I can work out. Until then, you think you can manage to get the work done?"

When Jerry is gone, Iris and Hazel look each other over.

"If you want to go on, I'll finish up this room." Iris, for once, doesn't smile.

"No, you go. I'll do it."

"Suit yourself." Iris shrugs and moves off.

Finally, with the room to herself, Hazel begins to relax. She moves around the periphery, thinking about Mabel Becker. She remembers Mabel had a role once in the town melodrama, played the heroine who gets tied to the tracks. She had pretty gold hair then. Hazel sits on the edge of the bed and runs her hands over the pillow. There are one or two cards left. Hazel reads them, sentimental drivel, drops them in the wastebasket. She opens the drawer of the bedside table and takes out the copy of the Bible provided by the Gideons. Inside the front cover, where she saw Mabel tuck it one day, she finds a photo of Mabel and Barney. Both of them smiling, their heads tilted together, in front of Mount Rushmore. On the back, in Mabel's handwriting, *50th anniversary trip*. Hazel studies their faces, memorizing Mabel's, then slips the photo in her pocket. *I can't live without you*, Barney had written. But he would.

REDEEMING THE TIME BEING

Emily and her mother face each other across a narrow table in a foreign café. Annie, who never drinks coffee, has taken to it here in Spain, orders *café manchado*, a shot of espresso with milk and sugar. She says she likes that it's served in a tiny ceramic cup, not in a 14-ounce cardboard container like the lattes she's tried back home in Lincoln, Nebraska.

They don't look alike, this mother and daughter. Both are tall and thin, but Emily has the androgynous figure of a teen model, all legs and no hips. Annie's short, gray-peppered hair waves away from her face. Emily's blond hair stands up a half-inch long, a new style she hoped would shock her mother. Instead, Annie can't stop talking about how gorgeous Emily looks, how the buzz cut plays up her eyes.

"What shall we do today?" Annie peers over the brim of her coffee. Her hands cradle the cup, evenly trimmed nails on long fingers.

"I don't know, Mom. What's left to see?" Emily doesn't mask her annoyance.

"How about your new apartment?"

"I don't think so. Bea and Nieves are both gone over the holidays. I hardly know them. I don't feel right about going there."

"Can't we just peek in? I'd like to be able to picture you there next semester."

Emily shifts in her chair. Bites her ragged fingernails. "If I'm here."

"Of course you'll be here. We've been over this."

"You've been over it."

"It will get better. If you leave now, you'll miss out on the best part of the year."

They sit without speaking for a few minutes. Emily's foot jostles up and down under the narrow table. She hates it here. She's staying at a hotel with her mother during the Christmas break because she moved out on her host family. She couldn't take the blaring television, the old man and woman yelling at each other, the grandbaby crying. They gave her their best room, clean and Spartan, with a little girl's pink bedspread, a framed photo of Monica the saint, their previous exchange student who did nothing but study all day. Emily made herself eat disgusting food, *jamón* and something that tasted like bacon fat. She didn't know until two months into her year abroad that other Spaniards eat vegetables. She tried once to buy a tomato from a street vendor, but somehow purchased a postcard of the Virgin Mary. There are Virgins everywhere, garishly painted and plastic, some with blinking neon eyes, others spitting water from kewpie doll lips. One, in the doorway of a shoe store, holds out supplicating arms.

"Emily. You're making me nervous."

"Sorry." Emily presses her hand on her knee to settle her leg in place. She studies her mother, the familiar face, little makeup, softening skin, intelligent eyes. "Do you think about him?"

"Of course. You know I do."

"I keep seeing him in that hospital room."

"There was nothing we could do." Annie's voice sounds small and far away. There's a note in it Emily has not heard before. She's aware that there are many things about her mother she's noticing for the first time. For instance, when did she lose ten or fifteen pounds? Why does she take so long in the bathroom getting ready for bed at night? When did she get so tense, so anal? Annie showed up in Seville with a guidebook, all the famous tourist places underlined. In five days, they've been to the Alcazar, the cathedral, the Plaza de España, and several small art galleries. They've walked the halls of the old tobacco factory where Bizet set *Carmen* and where Emily theoretically attends classes at the Universidad de Sevilla. It's not the season, or her mother would have them attending a bullfight.

"I've been offered a sabbatical." Her mother, changing the subject.

Emily feels her gut wrench. "Really?"

Her mother does this. Trots off somewhere in the middle of every important moment in Emily's life. The year she started junior high, her mother was in India, researching the influence of Indian culture on British literature. During Emily's prom, in London accepting an award for her definitive book on the Brontë family. She never takes Emily with her. Emily's father wasn't able—or willing—to leave his architectural business to travel for months at a time, and her mother didn't want to be saddled with a child in a foreign place. No wonder she insisted that Emily do this year abroad. She wanted her out of the way so she could plan her next academic adventure.

"For next year," her mother says.

"Where would you go this time?"

Her mother puts down her cup, looks at her. Sighs. She opens the small bag she wears around her neck and fingers through her wallet, counting pesetas to pay the bill.

"We can talk about it later," she says.

Not caring that she sounds petulant, Emily says, "I don't want to spend our last day doing touristy stuff."

Her mother doesn't even pause. "Okay. You decide."

Emily looks out the window of the café. Suddenly she's tired. She wants to go back to the hotel, curl up on the bed, and face the wall. Instead, she says, "We could go hear flamenco."

"Terrific. When?"

"It starts about midnight."

Annie glances at her watch. "Only fourteen hours to wait. How about if we go shopping in the meantime?"

They're in an Andalusian lace shop, the last place Emily wants to be. Her mother embarrasses her, spouting out a few words left over from high school Spanish, the woman behind the counter humoring her. Emily believes all these shopkeepers hold tourists in contempt, especially Americans with their loud voices, sloppy sweatshirts, big white and neon flashy tennis shoes. The clerk looks elegant in a simple black dress, black leather shoes, her hair swept into a chignon. Emily guesses she may be older than her mother.

"Mom," Emily whispers into her mother's ear. "Let's go."

Annie has somehow managed to communicate which laces she's interested in, and the clerk lifts down bolts of ivory, white, ecru, off-white, linen-white, beige, cream, and natural lace. "Emily, look." Annie holds her hand beneath the delicate fabrics, the pigment of her fingers highlighting the detail of the woven patterns. "Let's buy some for your wedding gown."

Is she kidding? "Mom, I don't even have a boyfriend."

Her mother ignores her. "Doesn't it make you think of Jane Austen?"

"I'm not getting married." Emily thinks this is the truest thing she's said to her mother since she arrived in Seville. Why get married? Over half end in divorce, and of the percent that make it, one of the partners ends up alone. Why would she want to risk that?

Her mother tugs on her sleeve. "Emily, do you like the purer whites or these off-whites? Some of them tend toward gray and others more yellow? Look. Cool or warm. Let's see which goes better with your skin."

Emily dives deep inside, her body twitching to run from the store, knock every bolt off the shelf, and wound her mother in the process. But the clerk is watching, so instead, Emily stands silent and stiff while her mother makes gross grammatical errors speaking in halting Spanish phrases and drapes lace after lace over her shoulders.

Eventually, Annie settles on a heavy ivory lace, the cut pattern floral but indeterminate. Emily winces when her mother hands over her credit card. Annie has chosen one of the most extravagantly priced laces in the shop, and she asks for five yards.

"Mom, we're not talking about a tent."

"Emily. Be still. Let me do this."

They get out of the lace shop and trudge down the street. Emily walks fast, leaving her mother steps behind. She needs to kick a dog. Smash a window. Step in front of a bus.

At the entrance to their hotel, Emily crushes through the door, slams up the stairs, not waiting for the elevator or her mother. She unlocks the bolt and throws herself facedown on her bed. When her mother enters the room, Emily does not move. Annie crosses to the window, looks out at the plaza below, hangs her jacket in the closet, careful to arrange the shoulders evenly on the hanger. Emily waits for her mother to sit down by her on the bed. She anticipates the moment when her mother will ask what's wrong, and by God, Emily will tell her. She rehearses the rant—you don't ask me if I want lace; you don't ask me if I have any intention of getting married; you don't ask me if I want to stay here. What about me? What about what I want?

Instead, Annie sits in the chair by the window and opens a book. Unbelievable. Emily shudders, her body trembling, electric beneath the skin. She hates her mother, hates her, and why won't she come over to the bed and hold her?

The room grows darker as daylight wanes, and Annie does not move to turn on the lamp. Eventually, Emily tires of waiting for her mother to stir. She props on the edge of the bed and blows her nose in a tissue. Her mother sits in the shadows by the window, head down, the book open in her hands.

"You know what I really hate about being here?" Her mother doesn't answer. Emily talks to the silence. "I hate the way it smells. There's horse manure all over the streets. People throw rotting garbage out."

No response. Emily goes on. "In that house, I had to eat pork fat. The rind. And some fish stuff that tasted like sewer."

Still nothing. "They didn't even try to like me. They expected me to sit at my desk every night and study. They didn't want me to go out."

"Did you go out?"

Emily perks up. "Yes. I went out and stayed out late. I walked home alone across the river. I drank cheap wine with hundreds of strangers in the plaza."

"Good."

"Good?" That hardly seems like a mother response. Back in Lincoln, her mother would have had a fit if she stayed out late drinking. With strangers!

"What do you want me to say?"

"I want you to act like a mother. My mother."

Annie closes her book and lays it on the desk. Rubs her hands across her eyes. Emily feels a pang of guilt. How sad and small her mother looks.

Annie's voice falls into the gap between them. "When my father died, I was only a little older than you are now."

"Yeah, but he was sick a long time."

"You think that makes it easier?" Her mother's voice flares. Emily shrinks back on the bed. Everything she says seems to go wrong.

Annie takes a deep breath and begins again. "I went with your grandma to that café out on the highway in Reach, remember? Oasis, I think it's called. Some of the widows from the church were there, Corrine, Louise, you don't know them. We sat down. Corrine leaned across the table, looked Grandma in the eye, and said, 'You know the deal, Iris.' Grandma nodded her head. 'I know the deal,' she said. Later I asked her what Corrine meant, and Grandma said, 'Keep busy.'"

Emily waits, expecting more. Expecting something that makes sense.

"That's it? Keep busy. That's the best you can do?"

"We're looking for reasons. Everybody is, all the time, but us more than ever before."

"What kind of reasons? Reasons Dad died?"

"No, darling. Reasons not to give up." Annie stands, then, and turns on the desk lamp. "Now, let's get dressed in something fancy and go out for tapas. By then, it should be time for flamenco."

The crowded flamenco bar lifts Emily's spirits. They are led through a series of rooms, crowded with drinkers and laughter, to a back room set up with long tables and benches, the roof a lattice of scarlet bougainvillea. Emily loves the disorder, the bumping and shoving, the singer's lament cruising over the tops of heads. The young guitarist has dreadlocks and scruffy jeans. The older singer wears black pants, a white shirt open at the throat where he lays his hand over his heart. At the height of his performance he stands, arms gesticulating wildly in front of him. Emily's emotions soar with him, and out of the corner of her eye, she catches sight of her mother. Annie's not watching the flamenco artists. Instead, she's staring at the table next to theirs where a young man is cooking a sausage over a blazing ceramic bowl.

Afterward, on the way back to their hotel, a man accosts them in the street. With little crime other than petty theft, Emily has learned not to be afraid here, but she senses her mother's tension. Emily takes her mother's arm. She listens intently to the man, who talks fast while waving his arm up and down the street. She tries to walk her mother away, but the man follows them. Emily struggles to understand.

"I think he's got us confused with someone else. He says we've parked our car on this street. He says he owns this street and we have to pay him."

"Tell him we don't have a car."

"I did. But he says we do, and we have to pay him. I think that's what he's saying."

Emily watches her mother turn her head and look down the narrow cobbled street. There's no one in sight.

"Just give him some money." Emily wants this over with.

"Did you put him up to this?"

"What? No." Emily's stomach starts to clutch. The man seems larger, more menacing. A jagged scar on his right cheek screams of knife fight. Her mother keeps on smiling, oozing her ridiculous Midwestern charm straight at the man while she speaks to Emily.

"You did, didn't you? Part of your ploy to come home."

The man moves closer, his voice louder. Her mother grins like an imbecile. Before Emily can think what to say to convince her mother that they are victims of extortion, Annie glances away from the man to look at her. He seizes the moment to snatch her mother's purse. He sweeps it off her mother's neck, but her arm catches in the strap and the man shoves her hard while he yanks the bag free. Annie cries out, falls to the cobblestone street, and Emily stands frozen inside a cartoon cel, not certain if she should run after the man or tend to her mother. While she stares after him, he throws the purse down in the street.

"Mom. Mom, are you all right?"

Her mother has one hand against her head. Blood seeps through her fingers. Her other hand points down the street. "Get my bag."

Emily runs down the street, afraid her mother will disappear in the seconds that it takes to reach down and retrieve the bag. It's light. He's taken her mother's wallet. By the time she reaches her mother, Annie's standing, wobbly as a cheap three-legged stool.

"Did he take anything?" Blood drips down one side of Annie's face. She grabs the purse and squeezes it.

"We should find a hospital. You're bleeding."

"Head wounds bleed. It's superficial. Oh, God. He took my billfold." Annie's voice rises at the end.

"You might need stitches. We can ask at the hotel."

"It's not here."

Emily grabs her mother's arm. She's got to get her mother to a hospital. She's not taking any chances. Her mother wrenches out of Emily's grasp.

"I don't need a fucking hospital."

"Mom?"

"He took my billfold. Don't you understand?"

There, on the streets of Seville, her mother starts to sob. Horrified, Emily thinks her mother must have a concussion. She must be in way worse shape than she looks. She said "fucking." She's hysterical. She never loses control like this. Never. Not even in the hospital. Or at the funeral. Emily tries to remember what she learned in her high school health class about shock. She takes off her light jacket and wraps it around her mother's shoulders. Her mother trembles while Emily walks her over to the curb and gently presses her to sit. Emily lowers herself next to her and throws one arm over her mother's shoulder. By now, Annie has stopped sobbing, but she hiccups and gasps to catch her breath. No one has come by. In this crowded city, how could they have chanced upon such a deserted street?

Annie fishes a tissue out of a pocket and blows her nose. The bleeding on her head has abated, but her hair is matted with dried blood.

"Shit," her mother says. Even her voice wobbles.

"We can go to the embassy in the morning. Get a new passport."

Her mother shakes her head. "I don't carry my passport. Just a copy."

"We'll cancel your credit cards at the hotel."

"I don't carry those either. Not at night."

"What'd he get?"

"Cash."

"How much?"

"I don't know. Forty, fifty bucks."

That's it? Emily has seen her mother hand over more than that to homeless drifters. "So . . ." She can't think how to finish the sentence.

Her mother shudders. Emily feels it ripple through her like a tsunami. "Pictures," Annie whispers.

"Pictures?" Emily echoes.

Her mother shrugs. "You. Your dad. The three of us."

Every muscle in Emily's body hardens. She feels herself poised, a hunting dog sniffing strange prey. Something is way off-kilter here. "Aren't there copies?"

Her mother shakes her head. Sniffles.

"You carried one-of-a-kind pictures in your billfold?" This, the same woman who makes photocopies of her credit cards, leaves her passport in the hotel safe?

Annie only nods and breaks out into fresh sobs. Emily wraps a protective arm around her mom. Helps her to her feet. "C'mon," she says. "We're going to get your head looked at."

The hotel clerk rustles up somebody on the staff to inspect the gash on her mother's head. Emily suspects the man has no medical training, but he does clean the wound. It's ugly but not deep. He dresses it with antiseptic cream and a bandage and sends them up to their room. Emily and her mother don't say much. They're both spent. Emily waits for Annie to finish up in the bathroom before she goes in herself. When she comes out, her mother is asleep, her mouth slack and drooling onto the pillowcase. Emily stands over her a few moments, watches her breath rise and fall. The blanket has fallen away from her mother's shoulders, and Emily reaches down to snug it back in place. She throws herself onto the other twin bed, and before she can begin to think through the events of this night, sleep overtakes her.

The next morning they rise early so they can have breakfast together before Annie's flight to Madrid. She'll catch another to Amsterdam, then to Lincoln, a long travel day ahead. They decide to splurge and eat in the hotel restaurant. They are unnaturally polite, offering each other more coffee, cream, sugar, additional sweet rolls.

Eventually Annie clears her throat. Here it comes, Emily thinks. Here comes the speech. She's prepared to tell her mother she's coming home. She's already booked a flight. A lie, but so what?

"The sabbatical is not really a choice."

Her mother sounds—Emily gropes for the word—apologetic? "What do you mean?"

"Dean Ross thinks I need some time off. I'm not in the classroom this spring. I'm assigned to admin stuff. Research. At least that's the public line. He couldn't arrange the sabbatical any sooner."

Emily drops her gaze to the floor. The ground keeps falling away as she stares at the tile. She finds herself following the tiles until the floor meets the angle of the wall, up the wall to the ceiling. Not an earthquake, then.

"Wow," Emily manages. It comes out as a whisper.

Her mother nods. "Yeah." She reaches over and covers Emily's hand with hers. "I don't want you to worry. They can't fire me. I have tenure."

"Is it . . . is it that bad?"

Emily waits while her mother decides what and how much to tell her. Annie's teeth worry her lip. Her hand trembles. She looks past Emily at an apparition over her shoulder. Emily fights the urge to turn around and see what her mother is staring at. Finally, her mother returns to her.

"Probably not. I've known the dean a long time. He's looking out for me. I need some time to get it together. Get my focus back."

"Were there complaints?"

Her mother nods.

"From students?"

"I missed class a few times. Overslept. Sleeping has been difficult."

How is this possible? Her mother's classes have always been favorites; she's the star of the department.

"What . . . what will you do?"

"See a therapist, I expect. Try yoga. Take up golf. What other people do when bad things happen."

"No, I mean next year."

"I don't know, really. You'll be in your last year at Madison. I could go somewhere. London, maybe. I still have a few friends there."

"I could come with you."

Her mother dabs at her mouth with her napkin. She's buying time. When she does speak, her voice is pitched high and tight.

"Maybe it was wrong of me to insist that you get on with your life. I don't know. I didn't want you to be saddled with your sad sack mom."

"I'm sad, too, Mom."

"I know, darling. Of course you are. This happened . . . the timing was so bad, just when you are supposed to be enjoying your independence."

"This spring . . . I could come home." She means it, too. She could come home. And she would. Only now, she realizes that she doesn't want to.

"What about Bea and Nieves?"

"They're nice girls."

"Do you really hate it here?"

"It's been hard. Maybe it's me. I've made it hard."

"I'm sorry."

Emily answers quickly, staving off more sobbing.

"Me, too."

Emily's not sure what either of them is sorry for, but it seems the only thing to say. They're sorry for themselves, for each other, for the way things are.

"Your home will always be your home," her mother says. "I want you to know that.

"Okay."

"But, do you think it will be any easier at home?"

Emily looks down at her plate. She wets her finger and uses it to raise a pastry crumb to her mouth. Finally, she's ready to say what she must. "Will you . . . will you be okay?"

Her mother smiles, sits back hard in her chair. Lets out a long sigh. "I might come back. Around Easter."

Emily nods, afraid if she speaks, her voice will squeak like a rusty hinge.

"We could go north to Bilbao," her mother says. "How about Barcelona? Even Provence. You must have a week or so off."

"That'd be great."

"Something to look forward to." Her mother's voice sounds so wistful that Emily's chest hurts.

"But next year . . . ," Emily says, prepared to say she'll stay home or go wherever her mother wants to go. She could transfer to Lincoln, if it came to that. Or why not take some time and enjoy England with her mom?

Her mother waves her hand. "We don't have to decide now."

They drink more coffee, eat more pastries. They settle into an easy silence. Emily knows she's been allowed access to a hidden part of her mother's world. She wonders if this is what it means to be a grown-up. She doesn't quite have the language for it. It will be years before she understands that she is trading certainty and righteous indignation for ambiguity and compassion. Now, she knows only that she feels honored and strangely forlorn.

Back in the room, when she's packing the last of her bags, Annie holds out the bundle of lace. "Would you like to keep this with you?"

"You take it. Put it in a safe place. It may have to wait a long time."

Annie drops her head back and laughs. So quickly, there she is. The mother Emily has known. Emily swallows around the ache in her throat and waits, knowing this mother will say the perfect thing. And then she does. "We can always turn it into a tablecloth."

HARVEST

Marlene Gustafson stood with a smoking rifle cradled in her arms. Vernon lay in a heap on the ground, his body having pitched forward over the corral fence when she shot him in the back of the head. She thought he might hang up there, which made her cringe, the idea of him hooked on the fence like that, but he slumped down once the force of the blow subsided. She rolled him over with her foot so he'd be faceup. His head looked like a tire blowout, one side gone, exposed brain and bits of bone. Her nostrils quivered at the metallic tinge of gunpowder and blood. She reached down and straightened out his legs. He wore his best boots, handmade in Durango. She'd pulled them on him herself that morning, straddling his legs to get a grip. His right arm lay twisted awkwardly behind his back, but she decided to let that go. She didn't want to touch him more than she had to.

It was dusk, early May, and a full moon strained to rise. Marlene covered Vernon's body with a woolen blanket they'd bought long ago from a Navajo woman, hand-woven colors of the desert, sky, and sand. She stood over him a moment and watched the sun blister down in the west. The windmill creaked in the light breeze, and she snugged her sweater tight around her gaunt figure.

She left the rifle leaning against the corral fence and trudged up to the house. The screen door banged behind her as she stepped into the kitchen. She smelled the pot roast she'd put on earlier in the day. She walked across the worn green linoleum to a wall phone. They lived so deep in the Nebraska Sandhills that it cost her long distance to dial into Reach. She waited while the phone rang, wondering if everybody'd already gone home.

"Pinski, here," a voice said.

"Sheriff?"

"That's right."

"This is Marlene Gustafson, out on the Triple B."

"Oh sure, Marlene. What can I do for you?"

"Vernon's dead."

"My God. Do you want the coroner?"

"That won't be necessary."

"Who's your regular doctor?"

"What good's he gonna do now?"

"Well. There's cause of death to determine. Was it a heart attack?"

"No. I shot him."

"You . . ."

"I had to, Sheriff."

"Marlene, don't say another word. I'm on my way. And call yourself a lawyer."

Everybody knew Vernon Gustafson could be a mean sonofabitch. Marlene knew that herself when she married him. He hired on as a hand the summer she turned eighteen, and she saw the way he reacted when a calf broke loose or a horse wouldn't follow his lead. Once, he threw a calico kitten to the ground and broke its back because it nipped him on the thumb. He had a wild streak, but she was young and thought it manly of him to be impatient with fools. Besides, she'd hardly stepped foot off her father's ranch, what did she have to compare to? Her father rarely spoke more than five words at the supper table, and she'd watched her mother grow dim and gray and lonesome and nearly out of her mind with boredom. Then, her mother died when Marlene was but thirteen. That was no life for a young girl, out there, cooking for her dad and the ranch hands. She thought Vernon would keep things exciting. Her dad didn't like Vernon, and that appealed to her, too.

They were married in the living room of the house on a Friday morning, June 16, 1922. By evening she'd found out how hard a man Vernon Gustafson could be. He shinnied up inside her like he was taming a wild mare, bucking and bumping, and then he got off, leaving her bereft and sore. She limped to the bathroom in their hotel room in Cheyenne and washed the smell of him off her.

When she didn't come back to the bed, Vernon tapped on the door with his knuckles. "Marlene?" His voice was the softest thing about him.

She nodded but could not speak. She was afraid if she opened her mouth she'd cry, and she knew that would infuriate him. Sitting on the stool, she leaned her head against the cold enamel of the sink and shut her eyes.

He sat with his back braced against the door and told her about his life. He'd been raised by a man who believed his four sons were given to him for labor and no other reason. His mother died of pneumonia when he was five. He left home soon as he could get his legs under him, at fourteen. He was thirty now, and he'd never loved another woman. He'd known a few intimately, but she couldn't expect him to be a monk.

"You're such a little bitty thing," he said. "I never saw anyone as pretty as you. I didn't mean to hurt you, if I did."

She came out of the bathroom then. Her night shift skimmed her knees, peach satin with white eyelet edging. Narrow straps that slipped easily off her shoulders. He lifted her in his arms and carried her to a rocking chair. He sat with her in his lap, petted her and whispered to her, and by morning they'd found a way to be together that didn't make her quake in fear.

Not long after that her father died when his horse stumbled and fell down a ravine. She had no siblings; the ranch fell to her and Vernon, the two of them alone out there except for summers when they had to hire a few hands to help out on the place. Through the long winter months she sometimes fell into melancholy. While Vernon pitched hay or rode the fence line, she sat for hours and looked out on the bleak prairie, nothing or nobody for miles. Other times they lay together in the big brass bed. He stroked her body with a hand tuned to living things, and she quickened under his touch. Hungry to pleasure each other, they studied anatomy and the French pornography Vernon had saved up from his ranch hand days. He showed her how various animals managed, and they laughed and tried each inventive pose.

Over the years she got pregnant five times, and five times she miscarried. The first time tore her apart; the second nearly killed her. She caught Vernon sobbing in the barn, and they clung to each other. The third time, she half expected the slow leak of blood, and the fourth and fifth, she didn't bother calling the doctor.

She had Vernon and no one else. When branding time rolled around, she made small talk with the women who showed up with salads and pies, awkward and nervous, which they mistook for disinterest. No one knew her. No one knew if she was capable of murder.

The trial took place in Reach, the county seat. Onlookers packed the courtroom, despite the fact that it was located on the second floor of a courthouse built in 1865 and stifling in the August heat. Judge Hawley, under a heavy black robe, wore glasses that slid down his sweat-lined nose. The bailiff said the judge's back hurt from driving all the way from Kearney in a Buick with a weak suspension system.

Marlene's attorney, Drew Avalon, drummed his fingers on the oak table, his right knee jiggling up and down. He had a lot at stake in this case, his first murder trial. Drew had grown up in Reach and offended everyone with a sour valedictory speech on graduation night, calling his teachers narrow and his classmates hicks and rubes. Most thought he had a lot of nerve coming back home to set up a law practice. Marlene hadn't known another lawyer in town, so he'd been assigned.

Cecilia Parker sat in the third row on the opposite side of the courtroom from Marlene. She did not miss one minute of the trial, leaving her husband, Earl, to fend for himself on his lunch hour home from the John Deere Implement Company. She held her knitting in her hands and worked row after row of stockinette stitch into a shapeless blue sweater, eyes riveted on Marlene's face.

The ceiling fan whined. Out of balance, it clicked once during every rotation. Dill Harmon, the county prosecutor, sat under the fan and tried not to blink with every click. He was sixty years old, knew everybody in the surrounding region, including Marlene. She sat straight and prim on the witness stand, her natural shyness and years isolated up on that ranch making her look prudish and out of touch. She was guilty, no contest there, but the question was, why? Afterward, people would say Dill threw her a bone, hell, everybody knew he'd been in love with her once, too awkward to say so and scared off by her father.

"Marlene," Dill said, standing close to the witness box, one hand on the oak railing. "Did you feel that you just had no choice?"

She raised her chin. Still a pretty woman, that peppery hair and lanky figure. She shifted in her seat, pulled at the front of her white blouse to get some air moving. "No. I had no choice."

"No further questions," he barked. On the way back to his table, he looked over at Drew Avalon and nodded his head. Take it home, he seemed to say to those watching, especially Cecilia Parker, who believed all lawyers worked in cahoots. Everybody knew Cecilia despised lawyers and doctors, ever since her son died of a mistreated snakebite and the courts did not hold Dr. Metcalfe accountable.

It had been Vernon's idea for Marlene to go to town with bruises. He thought they needed to establish a pattern.

"You'll have to go alone," he said. By then, he wasn't being seen in public. His symptoms had progressed to the stage where he couldn't walk without help. She held a straw to his mouth for drinking. They'd driven to Denver for the diagnosis, and when she first heard it, she didn't know what it meant. Who's Lou Gehrig, she said.

Nobody thought that much about it when Vernon sold off their herd. They were getting up in years and had no sons to carry on for them. Vernon leased the land to their neighbors. People felt sorry for it, but the O'Briens were glad to have the extra acres.

Months later, Marlene and Vernon sat at the kitchen table. Vernon needed a dishtowel tied around him to keep from tilting out of the chair. Drool streamed from the sunken side of his mouth.

"Marlene, I can't live like this," he said.

She stirred fresh cream into his oatmeal at the stove, her back turned to him.

"I know it's hard," she said.

"You got to help me," he said.

She brought the bowl to the table and picked up a spoon to feed him.

"I'll tell you how to do it," he said.

She pressed her lips tight and looked out the window onto the prairie where wild grasses swayed and bowed to the wind. She'd seen plenty of animals put down; the thought wasn't new to her.

He raised one shaking hand and placed it on her arm, his eyes glazed and sad. "I've always loved you, darlin'."

She placed her hand over his, patted it.

"I want you to shoot me."

A shudder passed through her.

"I'll leave the place and time up to you."

Her tears fell on their clasped hands. She ran her sleeve under her nose.

"Don't carry on," he said.

She picked up the spoon. "C'mon, now," she said. "Eat your oatmeal."

At the trial Drew Avalon brought in Dr. Metcalfe, who testified that he'd seen bruises on Marlene in the last year. He told how she'd come into his office looking frightened, and he'd noticed the black eye, her upper arm showing thumbprints. No, he hadn't taken pictures. (Here, he fidgeted in his chair.) She came to him for indigestion. He supposed it was anxiety and prescribed an antidepressant. He'd asked her if everything was all right out on the ranch, and she said it was, and he couldn't make her do what she wouldn't do for herself, could he?

The pharmacist, Wade Pritchard, testified that she'd had a prescription filled. No, she hadn't had it refilled, but that wasn't unusual. People who lived so far from town often didn't get their prescriptions filled regularly, and anyhow, ranchers are a cussed, independent lot who don't like medication. (The crowd chuckled.) Yes, he had noticed the bruises around her eye and upper arms. No, he hadn't said anything to her; he didn't know what to say.

The minister of the Presbyterian Church, Reverend Finley, said he hadn't seen them for some time. He knew there was a deep sorrow over their lack of children. No, he'd never been out to their ranch. (Cecilia Parker snorted, and Judge Hawley rapped his gavel for silence.) They lived thirty-four miles up in the Sandhills, and he couldn't be absent that long from his responsibilities around town.

When it was Marlene's turn to take the stand, Drew Avalon looked at her with concern. He poked out his lips and let puzzlement and pity pour out his eyes. Marlene kept her answers short and truthful, like she and Vernon had practiced.

"Did Vernon give you that black eye?" Drew asked her, in his mealy-mouthed voice. She tried not to smirk. (In fact, she'd blacked her own arms and hit her face against a towel-covered door. Then, she braced Vernon's arm while she rammed her eye into his fist, so she wouldn't have to lie outright.)

"Yes."

Drew Avalon painted quite a picture, their isolation, her being an orphan, Vernon taking over her ranch. Drew made her sound helpless as a newborn calf, but she let that go by. Finally he turned her over to the prosecutor, and Dill asked that one question: "Marlene, did you feel that you just had no choice?"

She answered truthfully. "No, I had no choice."

Everything had gone just the way Vernon had planned. He told her she would have to admit she shot him (who else was there?) to avoid an inquest, or it would come out that he'd been sick. No jury would believe a sick man could batter his wife. Vernon said it was a hell of a thing that a woman could get off for killing a man who beat her, but she'd go to jail for helping him avoid suffering. He said if she'd cover his body, they wouldn't look too close, and he'd been right about that, too. Sheriff Pinski peeled back the Navajo blanket, saw the pulpy mass of Vernon's head, and turned aside. After that, Vernon's remains were cremated (no undertaker to study the body) in compliance with his will.

Marlene watched Dill walk back to his seat and felt the grip lessen around her chest. She gathered her feet under her, as if to rise, when Cecilia Parker stood up. Cecilia wore a flowered skirt and a tank top, her upper arms taut and speckled with brown spots from years in the sun. Her hair clouded in a tangle of curls atop a long body, like a nest crowning a fence post.

"Not so fast," Cecilia said. "I got something to say."

The judge pounded his gavel, commanded Dill and Drew to approach the bench. The bailiff took it on himself to escort Marlene back to the defendant's seat. The whole room buzzed like a disturbed hornet's nest, until finally the judge banged his gavel. "In my chambers," the Judge said. He pointed his gavel at Cecilia. "You, too."

There was nothing for Marlene to do but wait. The bailiff brought her water. She drank it slowly and tried not to worry. She couldn't think of anything Cecilia might say that would be incriminating.

She'd run into Cecilia on one of her visits to town before Vernon died. She'd gone into the drugstore for lotion and deodorant when she noticed a rack of garden seeds. She lingered over the packets of carrots, pole beans, peas, radishes. She loved growing things, but Vernon thought a kitchen garden was a waste of time, too much work for food he didn't care to eat anyway. He preferred canned peas, slimy and soft. She tried for years to garden, but Vernon resented the money spent on seed, hated the mess when she took to canning, refused to help spade the ground. She made pickles (dill, watermelon, bread and butter), but Vernon would not eat them. That day in the store, the loss of her garden cut so deep she had to hang onto the seed rack to keep from doubling over. Cecilia walked by (her cart filled with cotton swabs and hair dye) and then stopped.

"Thinking about a garden this year?" Cecilia asked.

"Oh, I don't know." Marlene smiled and shrugged, which would have been enough for most people.

Cecilia touched a painted fingernail to a packet of beet seeds. "I love beets, don't you?"

Surprised, Marlene said, "Yes, I do." Vernon hated beets. Said they tasted like dirt.

"Plant 'em by the moon," Cecilia said.

"What?" Marlene knew she sounded vague and floaty, like she

wasn't all there. Truth was, she'd been missing for years, though she hadn't known it until now.

"Plant beets with a full moon. Plant carrots when it's waning. You'll have a better yield."

"Is that so?"

"My father swore by it," Cecilia said. "*Farmer's Almanac.*"

When the courtroom reconvened, Cecilia took the stand. After she was sworn in, Dill stood to question her. He hitched up his pants, ran his fingers down the seam of his pants. His eyes moved around the room, glancing off Marlene, then the jury, to Cecilia, and finally fixed on the clock above the Judge's head. "Tell us what you know, Cecilia." No condemned man could have sounded more reluctant. The crowd held its breath and leaned forward.

"She planned the whole thing. I don't know about the law, but I didn't think self-defense could be planned."

Drew leaped to his feet. "Objection."

Wearily, the judge ruled. "Stick to what you know, Cecilia. We'll interpret the law."

Cecilia told the story, then. How she ran into Marlene, and they chatted about planting according to the *Farmer's Almanac.* Marlene knew lots of folks planted by the moon; she could sense the crowd's impatience, and her heart began to flutter with hope.

"That's it?" Dill asked, his voice incredulous.

"No," Cecilia said.

A small spasm clutched Marlene's stomach. She'd lost her nerve, that was the thing. She knew it was time, but she couldn't make herself do the job. She needed inspiration, and that's when she'd thought of Cecilia. She'd forgotten exactly what Cecilia had said in the drugstore. It was mixed up in her mind somehow, the red beets, the bloody act, the taste of dirt, and she wanted to get the timing right. Plant by the full moon, but what about harvest? Wouldn't this be more like harvest, when she ripped the beets from the ground, their roots dangling free, the tops already wilting as the living plant died, the red juice staining her hands no matter how many times she washed with soap?

She rang Cecilia in the middle of the day while Vernon napped upstairs. She knew the moon would be full in another night or two. Cecilia answered on the fourth ring. Marlene had to tell her twice who she was.

"What do you want?" Cecilia asked bluntly. Marlene had thought there would be small talk. She'd practiced for that, the lack of rain this year.

"I was wondering . . ." Her mouth was dry, her voice sounding like a squeaky pump.

"What?" Cecilia snapped.

"About harvest. Is there a phase of the moon for harvest?"

"Why're you thinking about harvest now? It's planting time."

"I know. I was just . . . I was planning ahead. Harvest. For beets. What about the moon?"

A long pause shivered on the line. Marlene held her breath, afraid Cecilia would either know too much or refuse to answer. To her relief, Cecilia seemed only to be thinking it over. "I'd say full moon. Same as planting. Can't go wrong with that."

"Thank you." Marlene hung the receiver quietly.

She pondered for two days whether she needed to do the deed in the moonlight, but she gave that up. Vernon would suspect if she tried to walk him out to the corral after dark, and he had orchestrated this to be a surprise. So dusk it was, on the evening of the full moon. She'd propped the rifle against the barn, out of sight. She helped Vernon get situated hanging onto the fence, looking out on the land he loved. She patted him on the back, her hand lingering between the shoulder blades. A lone meadowlark called across the prairie. She said she had to run up and use the bathroom. "Go on," he said. She didn't move. He nodded to her, his gray eyes probing and kind, and said again, "You go on now."

She left his side, picked up the rifle, pointed it at the back of his head, closed her eyes, and squeezed the trigger.

Marlene listened while Cecilia told Dill and the judge and the jury and the courtroom full of townsfolk about that phone call. She said she'd thought it mighty strange at the time, and then a few days later, when the moon was full, Vernon got himself shot.

Dill called Marlene back to the stand. Watching him fidget, Marlene recalled how he once stood on her front porch, ran his hands around the brim of his hat, her daddy watching from the front room. She tried to send a message to Dill without talking, the way she could with Vernon—*None of this is your fault*—but Dill kept on looking miserable.

"Did you make that phone call, Marlene?"

"Yes. Yes, I did."

A collective jolt vibrated through the crowd.

"Did you plan on killing Vernon at the time?"

Marlene hesitated. She didn't like people thinking Vernon was a wife-beater, but it was what Vernon wanted. He didn't want her to go to jail. He would have hated people knowing he was sick and weak at the end. Strictly speaking, it was Vernon who planned everything. She didn't know, when she called Cecilia, that she would shoot Vernon, with the moon. She looked at Cecilia, tried to read her face, but couldn't. She knew people didn't like Cecilia, thought her strange, her ways too witchy. When Cecilia first stood up to make her claim, even Drew had whispered, "Crazy old bat," under his breath. Marlene couldn't gauge what the crowd thought of her. She didn't know what the jury would do if she pit her word against Cecilia's, but having convinced herself it wasn't an outright lie and responding to a lifetime habit of putting Vernon's needs first and reasoning that she couldn't do much to damage Cecilia's already sullied reputation, she answered, "No, I couldn't say that I did."

Weeks after the acquittal, Marlene threaded her way through October grass to a small cemetery tucked behind a knoll on her land. She'd buried Vernon's ashes here alongside her ancestors. She stood before Vernon's grave, then stooped, picked up a handful of dirt, and sifted it through her fingers.

"Vernon." She spoke out loud, needing to hear a voice in that vast space. "I loved you best I could." She stood a while longer, until the chill air made her bones ache. "But you never let me have beets. Wouldn't adopt a child, neither. You never asked what I thought. Even about this last." She looked out across the prairie and heard the killdeer and mourning doves. She leaned forward then, as if to tell Vernon a secret. "I never stopped to think about what I wanted. Never did. Never knew how."

She walked out through the gate and stopped to loop the barbed wire over the fence post. Looking back at Vernon's grave, she lifted her hand, a small salute, and let it trail wordlessly through the air.

Marlene got through the fall and winter in that house by herself. She wandered the rooms, not knowing whether to sit in Vernon's chair or avoid it. She moved out of their bedroom and into the guest room across the hall. She read mountains of books, crocheted four afghans, painted a mural on the bedroom wall of palm trees and oceans she had never seen. She memorized recipes and psalms from the Bible and poems by Wordsworth. She made a few trips to town for supplies but talked to no one. Radio news, saturated with the Cuban missile crisis, left her disconsolate and jangled. Unprepared for the crushing weight of her loneliness, she thought of Cecilia Parker with something like longing. All through that winter, she heard the echo of Cecilia's last phrase in the courtroom, *Vernon got himself shot.*

When spring came Marlene baked a rhubarb pie. She rolled the crust thin, crimped the edges, poured cream over the top to brown. She drove into town and straight to Cecilia's house, parked on the street, and trod up the walk with her pie. Before she lifted her hand to knock, the door opened and Cecilia stood there.

Cecilia tilted her head back and raised each eyebrow into an inverted V. "You," she said.

Marlene did not flinch.

"You planned to kill him," Cecilia said. "On the night of the full moon."

"Harvest moon," Marlene said.

"A harvest moon in May?" Cecilia's voice rose. Marlene could not tell whether Cecilia was truly dismayed or mocking her, but she nodded.

"That's all you got to say?" Cecilia asked.

Marlene glanced out across Cecilia's yard and down the years of her life with Vernon. She thought she caught a glimpse of herself, a straight-backed girl who did not stop or wave but kept on walking, long braids swinging down her back. "You don't know," she whispered, thinking to prepare that young girl, to shore her up for the full cup of life.

Cecilia, overhearing, said, "I guess you had your reasons."

Marlene looked into Cecilia's stern face. "I baked you a pie," she said.

Cecilia sighted down the line of her long nose. She looked at Marlene's face and then at the pie. Marlene waited, scarcely breathing.

"Well," Cecilia said, swinging the door wide. "No sense letting a good pie go to waste."

They sat to the pie, two women on yellow chairs at the laminated kitchen table. Through the open window Marlene smelled the green of spring and the sweet scent of lilacs. She raised a forkful to her mouth and could not remember when food had tasted this good, this clean and nourishing.

SOLITARY CONFINEMENTS

Ted Brenner approaches his parents' home in Reach, Nebraska, with a confusing mix of dread and longing. He's driven from Minneapolis, a trip he makes once or twice a year. On the way up the walk, he reminds himself to unclench his teeth and shakes his shoulders loose. He sets his foot on the crumbling front step, his hand on the screen door. He notices a tear in the screen, serious business in a river town thick with mosquitoes. His fingers grope to close the flap, and he glances through the side window of the house next door. Through a gauzy curtain, he glimpses Mrs. Redmond's iron lung.

His father's at the door, grabs him in a bear hug, pulls him inside the house that smells. Jesus, it's worse than last time. His dad holds him at arm's length, his eyes sagging and rheumy, shirttail askew, unshaven. Worse than Ted imagined.

"Dad." Ted's voice sounds low and liquid, maybe his best feature, or so he's been told. "Dad. Dad, it's all right." He pats his father on the arm, straightens his collar.

When his dad has settled down, Ted lets his eyes stray around the room.

"Where is she?"

"Sleeping in the back bedroom. She's been restless all day."

"Did you tell her I was coming?"

"'Course I did, Teddy, what do you think? But I don't know. I don't know."

"Dad, why don't we sit down?" Ted takes his father by the arm and steers him to the ragged recliner in the living room. He sweeps a pile of yellowed papers and outdated magazines off the coffee table and piles them in a corner. His fingers leave trail marks in the dust on the table. He opens the sun-stained drapes to let in the afternoon glare. Dust dances in beams of light. One of his mother's robes, pink chenille with yellow roses, lies sprawled across the rocker. When he sits on the corner of the tweed couch, his hands brush against dried bread crusts that have fallen into the cracks between the cushions.

He's not been seated long when his mother drifts in from the back bedroom. Her gray hair sticks up in matted tufts. Dreadlocks, Ted thinks, but it's all wrong. The whole scene is bent somehow. There's his once beautiful mother, her lilac robe buttoned crooked, her mouth painted with wild cherry lipstick by a child who can't stay in the lines, and when his father takes her by the arm and leads her to him, Ted smells her body.

"Here's our Ted," his father says.

Ted's mother looks at him with vacant eyes. Her nervous hand paws at his father's arm. From somewhere out of the distant past, she drudges up her manners. "Welcome to our home."

Ted says the only thing on his mind. "Dad, when was the last time you gave her a bath?"

In the yard the next day, Ted works off some energy. He prunes bushes, pulls up old tulip stalks that haven't bloomed for years. He plans how he'll drive to Scottsbluff and buy some annuals. Petunias, maybe. Geraniums, hot red ones. In June there won't be much left, but anything will be better than this weed patch.

He left his father sitting at the kitchen table. Walked out on him, to be exact. Same old argument. Ted wants his dad to put his mother in the nursing home. He's worried that she'll fall or die of infection or get food poisoning. His dad can barely take care of himself. The house is filthy, she's unwashed, the ceiling of his old room bearded with cobwebs. His father won't hear of it. Damned old stubborn fool.

Ted tugs at weeds and straightens to stretch his back. He looks into the side window of that house next door. The curtain hides everything in shadows, but still he can see the outline of the iron lung, a lime stationary rocket Mrs. Redmond sleeps in every night to ease chest muscles weakened by childhood polio. He shudders. Once, he and a bunch of his friends, fifth or sixth graders, were playing at Roddy Willenbeck's. Willenbeck's Mortuary. Roddy's parents had gone somewhere, and the boys unlatched the basement door where the caskets were displayed. Ted can't remember now whose idea it was to crawl inside a coffin. Maybe he did it on a dare or to prove something to himself. He can see the ivory pillow and feel it smooth against his cheek. A luxury bed, his nerves jangling, something like pleasure creeping along his thighs, and then the other boys closed the lid. They didn't open it until he was sobbing, and then they called him a crybaby. Nobody, he decided then, should ever lie in a coffin, dead or alive. Cremate me, he has instructed Harvey.

Now, standing in his parents' garden, tulip greens limp in his hands, peering through gauzy curtains at an iron prison, fear climbs up his spine. He bends and yanks at baby ragweed, lamb's-quarters, clover with its tendril roots, not caring that the weeds rip his hands bloody.

At the supper table, Ted struggles to make conversation. His mother's in the back bedroom, feet lifted, eyes attuned to a flickering screen. Her hands knot and unknot, her toes flutter together. Ted doesn't need to be there to sense her agitation. He waits for his father to ask about Harvey, but he doesn't. Ted volunteers information about the coffee shop he owns, but his father only grunts. Finally, Ted asks about the Redmonds next door.

"They're getting along." His father says this with a dismissive wave of his hand.

"What will she do if Will dies?"

"Same as the rest of us, I guess. Cross that bridge." His father mops up leftover sauce with a crust of bread. First, they fed his mother mashed potatoes, mashed green beans, baby food–looking stuff. Then they made spaghetti with sauce from a jar. His father doesn't want to waste any of it.

"Remember when the Hamptons lived there?"

His father looks at him like he's talking about stock markets or openings on Broadway, like he's way offtrack.

"C'mon, Dad." Ted can't leave it alone. "Remember how Mrs. Hampton used to undress in front of her mirror? Right there in that bedroom."

His dad raises his eyebrows. A chuckle rattles around in his chest and exits in a cough. He shakes his head from side to side. "I thought I was the only one noticed that."

"She did it on purpose. Turned on the light, stood in front of the window. You'd have to be blind not to see."

They laugh then, instant male camaraderie, bonding around the exploits of a vain and lonely woman. Ted feels vaguely ashamed, knows better, but what the hell, he'll connect with his dad any way he can. Then, without warning, his dad's eyes shimmer, watery. His lips, smirking moments ago, tremble and fall slack.

Ted busies himself with his coffee. He swirls his spoon around in the oily slick on the surface. His dad stands and moves toward the stove. He pours himself a second cup of coffee, stands with the cup and looks at the wall as he speaks. "I don't know what ever happened to Mildred. I haven't thought of her in years."

The next day, Ted is determined to buy his mother a new pair of shoes. He can't bear the run-over, black lace-ups she slides around in all day. He thinks an outing will be good for them. It takes all morning to get his parents ready, both of them in and out of the shower, his father shaved, his mother dressed. After an argument, his dad agrees that his mother should wear an adult diaper. Somehow, they manage to get it on her, only sticking the tape to her skin once. She swats at Ted's head and misses. Ted wants desperately to cut her hair, but he's afraid to get near her with scissors. Instead, he washes and blows it dry, styling it as best he can to fall softly around her face.

He loads both his parents in his red Mazda and drives to Scottsbluff, thirty-six miles through flat and cheerless prairie. His dad acts like a kid playing hooky. His mother keeps knitting and unknitting her hands. Ted chatters all the way there, exclaiming over Chimney Rock, holding his nose past the Minatare feedlots. You'd think he'd never been this way before, but he's filling a vacuum with anything at hand. Finally, they get to the strip mall in Scottsbluff.

His mother will not budge from the car. She flat out refuses. Worse, she's terrified. Ted tries to pull her out, but she wails and bangs on her head. His dad can't take it.

"I told you this would never work. Leave her be, can't you?"

Ted slams the car door on both of them. He stomps into the shoe shop, picks out three shoes, one tie-up and two loafers, two brown and one black. When a young man walks over, dark hair hanging long on the back of his neck, in scruffy blue jeans and a Soul Asylum T-shirt, Ted shoves the shoes in his face. "I need these in a seven medium, and I want you to come with me out to my car."

"Sir?" The kid backs away bewildered.

Ted presses. "My mother's out in the car. She won't come in. She's . . . she needs shoes. Please."

Miraculously, the kid goes with him. He brings a shoehorn and a loopy smile, charms Ted's mother who slips her feet willingly into all three pairs of shoes. Ted and his dad watch the transaction in amazement. She chats with the boy, asks about his plans. She smiles and dips her head, her old flirtatious self. Any minute Ted expects her to step out of the car and pirouette around the parking lot. After Ted has paid for the shoes and stowed the boxes in the trunk, while he's driving to the garden nursery, his mother speaks from the backseat.

"Who was that nice young man?"

"A shoe salesman," his dad answers.

"No, not him. That other one. The one with blond hair."

Ted works into the evening planting white and purple petunias in the front beds, potting geraniums. His expert hands work the mix of potting soil and peat moss. He bought more hot red geraniums than he knows what to do with. With Ted, more is more. His own backyard garden, an overgrown Eden, sprouts erotic blooms every half-inch. He lines the geraniums on the broken stoop, two to every step, both sides. Standing back to survey his effort, he glances toward the Redmond house. A lamp glows softly in that front bedroom. He sees now that there are portholes along the sides of the iron lung, hinged, so someone's hands can reach in to make adjustments. The whole thing reminds him of a bad scene from an S&M movie, the body held motionless while hands creep along its sides.

He feels in the pocket of his jeans for his car keys, pats his hip to make sure he's got his billfold. Before he goes back inside to face his parents, he heads downtown to the Waterhole. As soon as he opens the door of the pool hall, he's struck in the face by a heady atmosphere of smoke, the pock-pock of balls shot from cue stick to corners, men's laughter and hunkered quiet. There are only two women, one sitting at the bar, another at a booth in the corner, both with men whose hands play on the women's shoulders and necks while their eyes stray around the room.

Ted asks for a beer, Bud on tap, and sits on a barstool. He lets the alcohol soothe his throat, drinks a little too fast, orders another. He's working on a memory, his mother laughing up into his face. She puts her arms around him, and they dance in the living room. He's seventeen and spinning around the room with his mother when someone jostles his elbow.

"Sorry." Ted looks up into a meaty male face, scythe-shaped scar on the left cheek, hair dull brown and lank.

"Don't recognize me, do you?" Only the right side of the man's mouth moves. Ted struggles to see past the scarring to a face he might have known years ago.

"Junior? Junior O'Malley?"

"You're good." The man lifts his glass to Ted, tips his head, and drinks. Sets his empty down on the bar, motions to the bartender to give him another. "You always did have a good eye."

Ted gathers his body away from Junior, turns slightly on the bar stool, shifts his weight to rise. He's not up to hearing how Junior's life got wasted by a run-in with a drunk cowboy on the rodeo circuit. Now that he thinks about it, he's sure it was Junior who suggested the boys try out the coffins at Willenbeck's. Junior showing off. Even then, out to prove something.

"Heard your mom was sick," Junior says.

Ted turns partway back. He studies Junior for some sign of the old swagger. Junior rubs the back of his hand across his closed mouth. Slams his fist on the counter. Ted flinches. He's positive, now, that it was Junior who closed the lid on that coffin. Ted gets to his feet, tosses a ten-dollar bill on the counter.

"It's a bitch. My mom died two years ago." Junior stares straight ahead, seeing something ghastly from the look on his face. Ted wants out of here, badly.

"Cancer," Junior says.

Ted stands, unsure what to do. Junior's still facing over the bar. His belly, pendulous, snuggles up against it. He used to be a handsome guy.

"Take it easy," Ted says. He turns away, his feet headed toward the door. He hesitates with his hand on the doorknob. She made great ginger cookies. He could say that to Junior. Your mom made great ginger cookies. He glances back, but Junior's already into his next drink, his back shielding him from the door.

After parking his car in front of his parents' house, Ted makes a detour on the way up the front walk. He steps over the low hedge and stalks toward the Redmonds' window, open to let in the breeze. A night-light glows from a plug-in halfway up the wall, casting an eerie glow. This is the bedroom window from which Mildred Hampton used to show off her body. Mrs. Redmond has no body, only her head protruding from the hard, mechanical tube. The lung takes up most of the space, diagonal in the room, the feet toward the near corner. The head of the lung—Mrs. Redmond's head—is positioned so if she turned or was propped up, she could look out the window. Now her head is flopped to one side, toward Ted, mouth agape. Mr. Redmond must sleep elsewhere, on the other side of the house. Ted stares a long while, until his legs feel numb, waiting for something dire, but nothing happens. She goes on sleeping, and finally he turns away and rustles through the grass to the back door of his parents' house.

Lying in bed, Ted pulls the sheet up to his neck, then rests his arms down at his sides. He lies pinned to his bed, conscious of his breath heaving in and out, timing himself to see how long he can take it before feeling claustrophobic. Ten minutes. Twelve minutes. Not hours. How do people get used to this kind of confinement?

The next day, Mrs. Redmond appears in her yard. She walks haltingly to the knee-high hedge between their houses, and Ted rises to meet her. He stands with a trowel in his hand. She's wearing cotton pants, tan, a blue shirt. She looks normal, although she wouldn't win any races. White hair crowns her with light. Her skin, wrinkled like crepe paper, looks soft and downy. Ted wants to touch her, the way you want to pet a fluffy dog. They say hello. Ted can't think of what comes next, so he says the first thing that pops in his head.

"Still sleeping in the lung, Mrs. Redmond?" Immediately, he regrets mentioning it. Does she know he's been spying on her?

She pauses, cocks her head. Ted looks down, embarrassed.

"How's your mother?"

Ted shrugs.

"Got a nice young girl in your life?"

"Not hardly." Ted laughs. Too loud. He still can't look Mrs. Redmond in the eye.

"Your parents haven't given up on you, you know. They want grandchildren."

Ted winces. It still gets to him, the way his parents lie about him. Mrs. Redmond drops the marriage talk, and they discuss a program on orchids they both saw on PBS. He watches Mrs. Redmond struggle to breathe, listens to her list methods of cross-pollination, and thinks that he'd like to graft her to his mother. He's come up with hybrid roses this way; why not people? With his luck, he'd get it backward and end up with a mindless mother who not only couldn't breathe but also wouldn't remember to use the iron lung. Instantly, he's ashamed of himself, so he offers to prune Mrs. Redmond's hedge.

Over the next few days, Ted dusts, vacuums, scrubs floors, wipes down every inch of the bathroom with disinfectant. He fills the freezer with Healthy Choice frozen meals. He cooks dinner each night. He's a regular hive of activity, knowing none of it will make much difference in the long run. One morning after breakfast, he insists on changing his mother's dirty blouse.

"Leave her alone," his father says.

"C'mon, Mom. Let's get this nasty thing off you." Ted tries leading her from the table to the bedroom, but she balks.

"What does it matter?" His father hangs on to the table for support.

Ted drops his mother's arm for a moment and turns to deal with his father. He's suddenly frightened that his dad might drop dead of a heart attack, so he keeps his voice calm. "She's entitled to some dignity, Dad. That's all."

"You don't like looking at her. But this is the way she is."

"No. This is not the way she is. This is the way you allow her to be."

Ted coaxes her away then. He sweet-talks her into letting him change her blouse. This simple task takes forty-five minutes, and he's wrung out by the end of it. His father finds him flopped in a reclining lawn chair.

"She's resting," his father says. He doesn't sit. He stands by Ted's chair and rocks side to side.

"Dad, why do you have to do this by yourself?"

His dad runs his fingers over his face, ends by cupping his jaw in his hand. He looks to all four corners of the yard before he turns to face Ted.

"I can't give her up, Teddy. I can't be without her."

"The nursing home is only blocks away. You could visit every day."

His dad looks at him, presses his lips together, and says nothing.

"Why not hire someone to come in?"

"Strangers? It upsets her. You see that, don't you? It's worse having her upset. Takes me the rest of the day to calm her down. She still knows me most of the time. I wish you'd just leave us alone."

That night, Ted sits up late reading, trying to quiet his mind before worry sets in for an all-night visit. He's exhausted by being here. On their nightly phone call, Harvey hears the fatigue in his voice.

"What happened?"

"Nothing. I'll tell you when I get home. I'm leaving in the morning."

Restless, Ted steps outside to look at the night sky. He misses this panorama of stars in his life in the city. Searching for Orion, then the Big Dipper, he hears a soft moaning from Mrs. Redmond's window. Spent and wanting only to be alone, he convinces himself he imagined the sound, or a stray cat is patrolling the neighborhood. The sound comes again. Louder. Unable to resist, he moves over to the neighbor's window. Mrs. Redmond's head rolls side to side, a moan escaping here, there, and once, Ted's sure she calls her husband's name. Will. Where is the man? Why doesn't he answer? She's clearly distressed, her breath ragged.

Ted has no idea what he's doing, but he moves toward the screened porch in back. There's a hook on the screen door, but one good yank pulls it open. Doesn't anybody in these small towns ever think about burglars? It takes Ted only a few seconds to reach Mrs. Redmond's room. Knowing he will startle her, he steps around where she can see him and whispers her name.

"Mrs. Redmond."

Wild eyes, and he quickly stammers.

"It's Ted. I stepped outside; I couldn't sleep. I heard you moaning. Shall I get your husband?"

With clamped lips, she shakes her head no. She tries to speak, but her breathing is labored, and because he doesn't know what else to do, Ted steps to the top of the lung and places both hands on the sides of her face. He bends low and intones, "Shhh, all right now." He croons to her until she quiets and her breath evens out. When he's sure she's settled, he removes his hands, runs his fingers down the sides of his jeans.

"I should . . . I'll go now."

"No." She says it sharply, though her voice is barely audible. "Please. Don't. Not yet."

"Is there something . . . should I get you some water?"

She shakes her head. Tears pool at the corners of her eyes, run down her temples to spill on her pillow. Ted spies a box of tissues atop a small table, stretches his hand to grab one, wipes her eyes.

"Sometimes . . . I get panicky."

"Do you want out of there? Do you need help?"

She shakes her head again. "It's better . . . better tomorrow if I stick it out. There's a chair, there. In the corner."

Ted pulls forward a straight-backed chair and sits where he can see her face. He smiles. The chair is hard, uncomfortable, the back bordered with decorative knobs that gouge his back, but nothing compared to what she's dealing with.

"Mrs. Redmond . . ."

"Call me Flora." She raises one eyebrow and smiles. "I think we're on a first name basis, don't you?"

"Okay. Flora."

"I had . . . a bad dream. It comes, sometimes."

"The same dream?"

"Always the same."

"Do you want to tell me about it?"

Her eyes probe deeply into his. There's an intelligent light there.

"Too tired." She sighs and closes her eyes.

"Will you be all right, now?" Ted starts to rise.

"Talk to me." She says it plaintively, a request. "You have a lovely voice."

"So I've been told," Ted says.

"I'll bet you have." A low chuckle wends its way out of her wracked body. She must have been a hell of a woman in her heyday.

"Talk about what?" he asks.

"Anything. A bedtime story. Tell me about your life."

Ted talks. He tells her he lives in Minneapolis. Owns a coffee shop. At first, she murmurs from time to time, her eyes flicker open, but it's not long before her breathing deepens. If he stops talking, she stirs all over again, so he tells his life story. He doesn't forget testing the coffins in Willenbeck's Mortuary, the closed lid, though he leaves out the part where he compared the coffin to her iron lung, in case she's still listening. He mentions that he's gay and that his parents know but pretend not to. He came out to them during college. He's partnered with a wonderful man. His parents don't want Harvey in their home, and they won't come to Minneapolis. Even if they could, which they can't now, they wouldn't. His mother's sick. She doesn't know him. She doesn't know anything about him. Once, in Omaha, when he was young, he met a fellow in a bar and went with him to a hotel down by the Old Market. The guy made love to him, then beat him up, tied him naked to the bed, robbed him, and left him there. Too embarrassed to call out, he was there two days before a cleaning woman found him. He had to have stitches in his face. He was naïve and stupid and, well, ashamed. Of course, he didn't tell his parents. Harvey's Jewish, did he mention that before? His parents don't know that, either. Ted collects Polish glass ornaments. The first Christmas he and Harvey were together, Harvey made him promise he wouldn't put up any religious ornaments. That's okay, because he's not religious. But the new collectibles that year were the Three Kings. He drooled over them, but Harvey reminded him of his promise. He said, "Look, Harvey. Look at that ermine cape, the glittering jewels. What straight guy do you know who'd wrap a gift like that? Those aren't kings, Harvey. Those are three queens." They laughed and bought the ornaments. Isn't that a great story? But he can't tell his parents. They miss out on so much. They're waiting for grandchildren, but he's their only child and they're missing his life.

Certain that Mrs. Redmond is safely asleep, Ted stops talking, stands, and peers down at her. He'd like to kiss her brow. Touch her face one last time. He does neither. Feeling composed and strangely cleansed, he moves quietly from the room, gently closes the back screen door and under the canopy of stars and night, crosses over the lawn.

Ted has just eased himself under the sheet when he hears his parents' door bump open, recognizes his mother's shuffle in the hall. He gets up to check on her. Thinking this night may never end, he pulls on his jeans, buttons the fly while he looks in the bathroom, in the kitchen. He glances through the window at the house next door, the bedroom faintly glowing. He's glad, for some reason, that he can't see the iron lung.

He finds his mother standing in the middle of the living room, arms lifted, elbows and wrists slightly bent, fingers delicately curved. She's silhouetted against the window and the streetlight outside. Through her summer nightgown, sleeveless and sheer, Ted can see the sag of her breasts, her pillowy stomach, and yet, he's knocked out by her beauty. Afraid to disturb her, he stands and watches, and then she begins to sing: "Irene, good night, Irene, good night." She turns in perfect rhythm to the waltz. Somehow she misses the coffee table, the floor lamp. Ted knows it's only a matter of time before she bashes a shin, falls and splits open her head or, worse, breaks a hip. He knows he has to do something, but he loves seeing her like this, half in shadow, where he can remember the mother he once knew. He moves forward and lays both hands on her shoulders, his face inches from hers. She doesn't flinch, leans her weight into his hands, docile and smiling. If only she could die right now, while he is here, holding her, something painless and fast. He closes his eyes to conjure up a bolt of lightning, offering himself as the conduit. He discovers he's holding his breath when finally the need for air overcomes him, and he gasps. She shies, suddenly not trusting him, so he opens his lips and sings, "Good night, Irene, good night, Irene, I'll see you in my dreams," while he takes her by the hand and leads her down the hall. At the doorway to her bedroom she stops, but

Ted begins the song again, and they move in time, their bodies knocking together, to the side of the bed where he gentles her into sitting, then lying down, and lifts the sheet to tuck her in, lingering to make up for wanting her dead and because he doesn't want to let her go. Even like this, he longs to be near her.

His father snores on the other side of the bed, his face and body cling to the edge away from her. Ted stands and looks at the two of them lying there, rafts drifting apart on an ocean, an invisible filament binding them together, for better and for worse, and by God, if they haven't had it all.

The next morning, Ted rises early, makes himself coffee and toast. He kisses his sleeping mother on the cheek and hugs his dad in the doorway of the kitchen. He's cheerful because it's easier to leave that way. He gets all the way out to his car, stuff thrown in the trunk, when on impulse he goes back and picks up two potted geraniums. He crosses his parents' yard and moves over the grass to the Redmond house where he sets the two geraniums on the front step. He feels he should say something, a benediction, but he can't think of anything that doesn't sound trivial, so he stands a moment in silence, and then he's gone.

NORMAL

As an auctioneer's wife, Teresa Bailey thought she'd seen it all. Still, she'd never had a client whose household goods included an iron lung. Their best bet for a sale would be the Internet. Somebody, somewhere, would make an offer. Secretly, Teresa hoped for Steven Spielberg or some other movie mogul, who would pay outrageous sums for an authentic prop. She loved movies, herself. She and her son, Otto, sat many a Friday night watching films they rented. Otto, at fourteen, read all the reviews online. He didn't go in for action blockbusters, like most boys his age. He liked independent films, dark and twisted. Teresa worried about him constantly.

She knocked on Flora Redmond's door. If it were anyone but Flora, Teresa might have walked on in, yoo-hooing in a casual way, but Flora didn't invite that kind of friendliness. Flora answered the door in blue cotton pants, a floral knit top shirred over the bodice, silver hair immaculate. A small gold heart dangled on a slender chain around her neck. She wore tiny gold earrings in pierced ears. Teresa had dressed for this occasion, traded in her usual sweatshirt, blue jeans, and sneakers for a plaid blouse, tan pants, and loafers. Still, she felt frumpy in Flora's presence. Her hand traveled to smooth her wiry hair.

"Please," Flora said, "come in," her voice like whispers in a heavy fern wood.

Flora motioned toward a cream-colored couch. Teresa brushed at the seat of her pants before she sat. Hard telling what glop might have been on the upholstery of their van.

"Would you care for something to drink? I could brew some tea," Flora said.

"Just water. If you have ice, that'd be great."

Teresa wanted Flora out of the room so she could look around without seeming to pry. It had only been three months since Will died. Normally, Teresa would recommend waiting a year before making a decision to sell, but Flora was finding it difficult living on her own.

Teresa jotted notes on her yellow pad—couch, two chairs, a recliner, two lamps, a coffee table, an end table. An old upright piano in the dining room. Except for the iron lung in the front bedroom (which everybody in town knew about thanks to Glenda Barrenhorst, the welcome wagon hostess), all these furnishings were as ordinary as corn flakes. She'd expected, what? Something exotic. Telling, at least. Will and Flora had turned up in Reach late in life. Married. No children. No relation in these parts. When asked, they'd said only that they wanted a quiet life. There were rumors, of course. The most popular ones involved sordid crimes, not murder or assault but something crafty and lucrative, embezzlement maybe. Offshore bank accounts. Some folks said they'd been part of a cult and ran away under assumed names. Or they'd worked for the FBI or the CIA and were in a witness protection program. They had to be running from somebody or something. Otherwise, what were they doing in this backwater town?

Flora returned from the kitchen, set a glass on a ceramic coaster on the end table, then sat in a wooden chair with a needlepoint cushion. "All of this"—she swept her hand around the room—"will have to go. I'll have limited space in my assisted living apartment."

Teresa sighed. "The piano will be a tough sell. And the iron lung, but I've an idea for that."

"I'll have to take the lung," Flora said quietly.

"Really?"

"I sleep in it. Every night. Rebound effects from childhood polio."

Teresa scribbled a caustic note to herself. How could she have been so stupid? She thought polio was a thing of the past, like dial phones and leisure suits. She'd assumed the lung was a prop, a sentimental relic or a conversation piece, like a planter she once saw made from an elephant's foot. She spoke without looking up from her tablet. "Where will you go?"

"I thought Denver."

Teresa wanted to ask, why Denver? Why not Lincoln? Or Albuquerque? Or Toronto? If nobody cares—a terrifying thought—how would you decide where to spend your last days?

"You want everything else sold at auction?"

"Yes, all but the paintings."

Teresa raised her head from the pad. "Paintings?"

Flora's hand fluttered near her throat. She picked up the tiny heart and ran it back and forth on the slender chain. "I need help getting them crated and sent."

"Where?"

"I've donated two to the University at Lincoln. The others, three others, will be sold at a small gallery in New York."

With some effort, Teresa managed to work the hinge of her jaw and close her gaping mouth. She reminded herself to breathe. She knew how to act matter-of-fact about the damnedest things—pet graveyards in basements, rooms bursting with clutter, kitchen cabinets crusted with moldy food, gun cases shot full of holes, pictures with people's heads cut off. But really? First, the iron lung. Now this? She wet her lips and answered in her most professional voice. "Of course, Flora. We'll do anything we can to help you. Are you a collector?"

Teresa thought that was the proper word. Collector. Someone who could afford to buy important works of art. Her mind worked at lightning speed. Was it Flora or Will who bought up these paintings? And where were they? Why hide them? Were they bought as investments to hide ill-gotten gains?

"No, oh no," Flora said. "Nothing like that." Her hand fluttered again, inspecting the folds of her bodice. "These are minor works. Hardly a ripple in the art world."

"Oh." Teresa sagged. Not van Gogh, then. Or that crazy artist who flung dots on a canvas. She and Otto watched a film about him not long ago.

"Anyone I've ever heard of?"

"No. I'm sure not." Flora stood.

Teresa stood, too, not sure what to do. They'd hardly made a dent, and she was being dismissed. She hadn't seen the paintings. She couldn't even look up their worth on the Internet if she didn't know the artists' names.

Flora smiled. "I tire easily."

Teresa narrowed her eyes. "Of course." No arguing with that line. Crafty. Teresa made a mental note not to underestimate Flora.

Flora walked her to the door. Once through on the other side, Teresa turned. "You do still want us to handle your sale?"

"Of course, dear." With that, Flora shut the door in Teresa's face.

Teresa sped home with the news hot under her tongue. She couldn't wait to tell Otto; this was better than a movie. She supposed she'd tell Warren, too, but she already knew what he'd say. *So what? We aren't going to make anything off paintings being sent to New York.* Warren wouldn't recognize a good story if it bit him in the ass. When those Shackleton sisters died, he hadn't cared one bit when it was revealed that they weren't sisters after all but instead two women who'd lived together and shared the same bed. People thought he was discreet, but Teresa knew the truth. Warren just didn't pay attention to the details of people's lives. Numbers and sports were Warren's language, and little else interested him.

She walked into a familiar scene when she got home. Warren had Otto trapped at the kitchen table. A big man, he leaned over Otto like a looming crane. A bowl of strawberry ice cream melted on the table. "Son, if you want to be respected in this town, you got to go out for football."

Warren had been riding this horse since school let out in May, trying to goad Otto into playing football in ninth grade. Warren had been a star fullback. Watching, Teresa's stomach hurt.

"Dad, I don't want to play football."

"Just go out. Make some friends. Be part of the team. One of the guys."

Otto snorted. Teresa winced. "Hey, you two." She kept her voice light.

They ignored her.

Otto stared into his bowl of pink soup. "I'm not gay, if that's what you're worried about."

Warren stood back, surprise on his face. They'd never spoken about it, but hadn't they both wondered? She secretly thought Otto's life might be easier if he were gay. Wouldn't gay people stand a better chance of appreciating his artsy ways?

Warren looked away, out the window. Frustration oozed out of his ears. He raised his big fists and dropped them. "I want you to have friends. You have to get along with people."

Otto raised his head, a sneer curling his lip. "Like you and Mom?"

"What's that supposed to mean?"

"Sucking up to everybody so they'll give you their business."

That did it. Warren yelled about kids and respect and how his old man would have decked him if he talked like that. He yanked Otto to his feet. The plastic bowl clattered to the floor upside down, speckling the white linoleum with pink goo. Otto stood with his fingers in his ears, singing la-la-la and being the irritating little shit he turned into whenever his father was around. Teresa wedged herself between Warren and Otto, placed her hands on Warren's chest, shoved with all her might until finally Warren said, "Christ almighty," and stomped out. She cringed when she heard the back door slam, waited for the roar of his pickup, squeal of tires, before she turned to Otto.

Her son, the creative genius, stood itching his crotch with his right hand. His curly dark hair looked matted, unwashed. Circles draped under his eyes, because he spent half the night surfing the Internet. He had hundreds of Facebook friends and none in the flesh. She wanted to smack some sense into him. His father was right. This kid didn't stand a chance in the real world. What was to become of him? She saw her son's future laid out clearly. Helpless, begging for pennies in a subway station. Penciled drawings of cartoon cels taped to walls of a cardboard box where he spent his nights. Cold. Alone. She shuddered.

"Mom?"

She heard him calling to her, but she couldn't get past the winter snowstorm in her head. She stooped to pick up the upended bowl. Ice cream glued her fingers together.

"Mom, why are you crying?"

She wiped her nose with the back of her clean hand. Snot streamed across it. "No more movies."

"Mom?"

Gently, she set the bowl on the table and stepped around the puddle to pick up a dishrag off the sink. On hands and knees, wiping the floor, not looking at her son, she said, "I got other things to do on Friday nights."

"C'mon, Mom. He'll get over it."

"No. I mean it. Find a friend. Go out. Get drunk. Give us a reason to ground you."

"You know I'm not like that."

Her heart hurt, squeezed like hamburger in a press. She sat back on her heels and forced herself to look at her boy's contorted face. "Son, I'm not sure what you're like. Are you?"

Teresa got through that sleepless night by making a list of what she'd do to help Otto get normal. She could sense him sitting up, working the Web.

#1. Curtail his computer time.
#2. Make him get a haircut.
#3. Buy him some clothes that aren't black.
#4. Invite the Jergensons over; they have a son his age.
#5. Give up Friday night movies. Don't talk about movies. (She stopped to wipe her face with a tissue. Blew her nose.)
#6. (She cringed, but wrote.) Back Warren's plan to get Otto into football.

After that, she fell back on her pillow, exhausted.

A week later, Teresa stood in front of Flora's paintings. They didn't look all that special. Slashes of color, thick and pulsing and oddly disturbing. Five canvases in all. Two hung on common nails in the back bedroom, where Will had slept. The other three Flora dragged out of a closet. Nothing special about the framing either, white mats, white metal.

"Will wouldn't let me sell these." Flora wore tan slacks today, a peach and green floral shirt. "He switched them around every few months. He said he couldn't take looking at more than two at a time." A small ripple that might have been a laugh caught in Flora's chest, made her cough.

The signature on every painting was the same. Flora. No surname. For a brief moment, Teresa considered that there must be some other Flora, someone this Flora had been named after. How could this genteel, quiet, elderly woman have painted these slashing, angry, vibrating, highly sexualized paintings? That one looked like a vulva staring right at her. Teresa averted her eyes.

"Well," Teresa managed. "My goodness. I had no idea you were so, so"—she waved her hand in circles and finally sputtered— "accomplished."

Flora smiled. Her lips smiled. The rest of her face remained inscrutable. "Let's have a cup of tea, shall we, dear?"

They sat at Flora's dining room table. Teresa waited while the tea was steeped, poured, the chocolate cookies plattered. Lace tablecloth over oak, the teapot blue and white china. A ceiling fan hummed. Outside, the June temperature had climbed over ninety degrees. Teresa fanned herself with her yellow tablet.

Flora lifted a steaming cup to her lips. "I'd just as soon you not tell anyone, dear." Then, she sipped.

"Oh." Damn. Teresa had been halfway out the door, planning how she'd carry this message home, to the beauty parlor, to the bakery, to the vestibule of the First Baptist Church. She could make hay out of Flora's story: Mysterious Artist Reappears. They'd get a whole lot more traffic for the auction, not to mention what could happen to the prices if the bidding got competitive. She hadn't told Otto and might not have even now, given her recent resolution to steer him onto a normal path. But gosh, not to be able to breathe a word? "Why all the secrecy?"

Flora shifted her weight in her chair. Her gaze floated out the window, seeing past the lace curtains. "Will and I came here to get away from all that. It wasn't part of this life."

"I see." Teresa did see, reluctantly. Flora wasn't her first client with secrets. "Can I ask . . . why did you stop painting?"

"I suppose I didn't need it anymore. My health was declining. The fumes from the paint . . ." Flora waved her hand dismissively. "And Will came back into my life."

"Back?"

"We'd known each other as children. I lost track of him for a while. A good long while. Neither of us had married. He came to a showing of mine in Chicago. My last showing, as it turned out."

Flora poured herself another cup of tea. She took milk and sugar. Teresa, who hated tea, took hers straight, lifted the cup to her mouth and managed a tiny sip. The silence stretched out between them. Just when Teresa had almost given up hearing any more, Flora sighed and said, "When I was twelve years old, I found out that my mother had been raped."

Good God, Teresa thought, but she said nothing.

"I found out because Billy—we called him Billy, then—walked me home one day." Flora's voice went on, in fits and starts. She spoke in such an undertone that Teresa had to lean forward to hear.

Billy had red hair and freckles. He could make people laugh. He got invited to parties. Flora never did. Flora had lank brown hair, and it wasn't cut in what others called a style. When it got too long, her grandmother hacked it off with a pair of scissors, all in one hunk.

One day, Billy followed her after school. She forgot to lie about where she lived and just kept walking because they were talking about art. Billy had been places, Spain where Picasso painted, and France. He had seen van Goghs and Monets. Billy's family had money. By then, they'd reached the corner of her block.

"I have to go, Billy."

"Okay. Is this where you live?"

She pointed to the third house, the one with the broken fence, collapsed steps.

"See you tomorrow." Then he grinned and took off in the opposite direction. She watched him go for a while, and then went home. Grandma grabbed her arm the minute she was inside the door.

"What do you think you're doing, you little shit?"

"Ow. You're hurting me."

Grandma dragged her to the kitchen and plopped down in a chair, still holding onto Flora's arm. She bent it in a way that hurt. Gouged her thumb into Flora's tender flesh above the wrist.

"Ow. Ow."

"Stop sniveling. I'll hurt you more than that if you start whoring around with boys."

"He walked me home. That's all."

"You're just like your mother."

"Leave my mother alone." Flora could make her voice hard against Grandma if she needed to. She was almost as tall.

Grandma levered her arm until Flora sat in the chair next to her. Grandma leaned into Flora's face, big yellow teeth and sour breath. Flora thought of the witch in Hansel and Gretel, but immediately felt guilty because her grandmother had sacrificed her youth for her and her mother.

"Your mother got pregnant when she was seventeen."

"I know that."

"She followed your uncle Cyrus to the roller skating rink. Somebody was bothering her, so she left. She said Cyrus's friend, Joe-Joe, raped her in his own backyard."

"Mom was raped?"

"Oh, there was a trial and everything. The defense attorney said it was Aletha's fault. She sashayed around those boys, wiggling her hips. She got pregnant, and then she had you."

"My dad was a rapist?"

"You just watch yourself, young lady, or the same thing could happen to you. Boys only want in your pants."

Flora squirmed. Grandma still held her arm like a vise. "Not Billy. He talks about art."

"Hah! He doesn't give a flying fart about art. And if you don't get that, I'll have to lock you in the house for the next ten years."

Grandma's eyes were focused and sharp, beady, penetrating through Flora's skin.

Flora looked down. "Can I go now?"

"No more Billy."

Flora nodded.

Flora stopped talking. Her face had lengthened, the corners of her mouth drooped. Teresa stood, put her hand on Flora's shoulder. Then Teresa gathered up all the cups and saucers, the plate of cookies, and carried them to the kitchen. She stood for a while looking out the window above the sink. Petals had fallen off a peony bush, cushioning the ground pink. A solitary fly buzzed between the window and the screen.

When Teresa had composed herself, she went back to the dining room. Flora sat, cradling her forehead in her hands.

"I'm sorry. If it's too much . . ." Teresa could see that Flora's whole life had been too much. "I'll let myself out."

Teresa stopped to breathe on Flora's front stoop. Though the days were long in summer, she was surprised to find the sun still shining.

At home, tensions ran high. Otto didn't so much move through his days as slam through them. Doors, plates on the counter, shoes on the porch, books on the floor. Wherever he could make a statement. At night, propped against the headboard in their room, Teresa and Warren whispered about their son.

"He still hasn't talked to Coach." Even in these low tones, Warren's voice rang with accusation.

"How do you know?"

"Cuz I asked Gary. I ran into him in Jack & Jill."

"Maybe we should let up on the football."

"This whole town revolves around football. It's like snubbing his nose, if he doesn't go out."

Teresa chewed her lip. "The Polanski boy doesn't go out."

Warren rolled his eyes.

"He could get hurt."

"Hell. He won't play that much."

Then Warren reached around Teresa to switch off the bedside lamp, brushing her nipples and letting his lips rest against her neck. She had to admit; their sex life had improved. Nothing bonds like a common enemy.

Two weeks went by before Teresa found an opportunity to get back to Flora's. There was no rush since Flora's auction date was set for mid-September. Teresa had her hands full with the Tremain auction. And Otto. She had to ride herd on him to make sure he kept to the rules they'd imposed on him. To their surprise, Otto took a job. He hired on at Hardee's. He made a friend, some new kid named Quentin Strickland. What kind of person is named Quentin, Warren had said, but Teresa assured Warren that Quentin seemed normal. He wore baggy jeans and T-shirts. He slouched, unkempt and surly. Around her, he was largely inarticulate. A regular guy. They should be grateful.

Now, she and Flora were seated once again at the dining room table. Flora wouldn't budge on keeping her art activities secret. Too bad, but Teresa had to admit people weren't likely to care about an artist they'd never heard of, even if she did have a painting hanging in the governor's mansion in Lincoln, which Teresa found out by Googling Flora's name. She'd learned that Flora had showings in Chicago, Minneapolis, and New York. She'd disappeared from the art scene abruptly, and no one knew why.

"So," Teresa said, once the tea had been poured. "How did you get started painting?"

Flora scooted forward in her chair. Teresa leaned in to hear her. Their foreheads nearly met across the lace tablecloth. This time, Flora seemed eager to resume her story.

By the time her grandmother told her about the rape, Flora's mother was already institutionalized. Her mother had depression. Her mother heard voices. Her mother had tried to strangle her grandmother, and Flora had to hit her mother with a croquet mallet to get her to stop. After that, Grandma had her mother committed. Grandma said that was the best way; her mother could get the care she needed.

Flora took a series of three buses across town to visit her mother. She sat with her in a stale room, no curtains on the windows, tile floor. The walls bilious green. Her mother rocked on the edge of the bed. Her hair hung in dirty strings, the ends frayed where she chewed on it. She hadn't had a recent bath. Flora sat on a hard-backed chair, not too close.

"Grandma made spaghetti last night."

No response.

"I got my report card."

Flora knew that report cards were a big deal in some kids' households. She knew that a report card like hers (3 C's, 2 D's, 1 F, the F in math) would be a very big deal to kids whose parents were part of the PTA, the same ones who showed up for parent teacher conferences. She missed a lot of school. Often, she didn't feel well. Plus, she was needed to go to the store for milk and eggs, to pick up her grandmother's medicinal whiskey in the brown paper bag from Skip Jaffrey, take the rent to Herm Griffith, their landlord.

Flora liked riding her bike to Herm's because it was down a lane on the outskirts of Lincoln, and she passed a field with three horses. If she pedaled fast enough, so her grandmother wouldn't think she'd gone astray or gotten herself into what Grandma called a compromising situation, in which case she might be sent to her room or made to kneel on rice on the kitchen floor until her knees bled, she could take a few minutes to study the horses. A black one with a white blaze of lightning on its forehead, a reddish-brown one with four white stockings and a swayed back, and the third, her favorite, gray and dappled with stars.

She held the way they looked in her head all the way home—and then, after the supper dishes were washed, while Grandma dozed over an open book in her chair, Flora sat at a tiny desk in her room under the eaves and drew horses. She loved the way their manes flowed under her pencil. She practiced until she could make the three of them gallop across the page, graze under a tree, stand together like old friends gossiping. She observed their distinct personalities—the bold black, the timid red, and the affectionate gray—and found ways to bind those attitudes to the paper.

At school, though she didn't do well in math (having missed out on fractions), she could draw. "When you get to junior high, you can take an art class," Mrs. Jordan said.

Sitting with her mother in the institutional place for sick people, Flora said, "Mrs. Jordan said I could take art in junior high."

No response.

"She says I'll love it. 'When you get to junior high, Flora, you can take art.' That's what she says."

Flora got quiet and real still after telling this. Teresa waited in the silence. She could hear Flora's labored breathing. Shadows from the afternoon sun danced against the wall. Teresa was afraid Flora would pass out or have some kind of attack. After a while, Teresa said, "You've had a hard life."

"Some of it," Flora said. "Some of it, I got real lucky."

"I'd like to hear about that lucky part." They both chuckled over that.

Otto took to going out on Friday nights with Quentin. Teresa and Warren stayed up late, worried and waiting. They pictured their son lying at the bottom of a ditch or passed out in the backseat of Quentin's car. They'd never met Quentin's parents. The Stricklands attended the Presbyterian Church. Quentin's dad was a manager at the ethanol plant. His mother had been a yoga instructor, but there wasn't much call for yoga in Reach. She was skinny and fit, just what you'd expect.

Otto had an 11:00 p.m. curfew, but he invariably walked in ten or fifteen minutes late. This became the territory of their arguments. They knew Otto did it on purpose, just to rankle them, and it did rankle them because it was calculated. They couldn't let it go, but it didn't seem serious enough to ground him.

He stopped banging around the house. He grew secretive and quiet. He slinked in and out of rooms, as if they weren't present. Even when they spoke to him, he reacted as if he hadn't heard or as if they were calling to him from some distant place he'd forgotten. He spoke in grunts. He wore slouchy clothes, ill-fitting jeans that impaired his natural grace. His walk became a stutter, his voice guttural. He slept a lot, when he wasn't working. The slack skin under his eyes looked bruised. His face took on an unnatural pallor.

One morning in late July, Teresa and Warren were sipping coffee over a Saturday morning breakfast. They kept their voices low, not wanting to wake Otto. He'd been late, again. There had been shouting, some shoving. If asked, they would have said Otto needed his rest, but the truth was that neither of them had the energy to confront their son. Teresa had planned to make waffles, but instead they were eating toast with peanut butter. Warren's jaw hung slack. He was growing older before her eyes. Teresa knew her hair looked ratted and wild.

"Don't worry about it," Warren said. "I was exactly the same way at his age."

"You were?" Teresa found this hard to believe. At fourteen, Warren was sitting beside his daddy in the pickup, learning how to do the auctioneer's prattle by selling off telephone poles on the side of the road.

"Sure. It's normal for a boy to sow some wild oats."

Teresa stood. She moved over to pour more coffee.

"Normal," she said. Then, with more force, "Remember how we worried when he kept bringing home those dead birds, conducting funerals in the backyard?"

"Yeah. We damn near drove ourselves crazy over that one."

"He got over it."

"Right." Warren knew his lines. "Then, when he told his teachers he was a descendant of Black Elk. Remember that?"

She laughed. Actually laughed. "Oh, yeah. We thought we had a compulsive liar on our hands."

"How about that imaginary friend?"

"Sir Edwin. That was during his knights and dragons stage." Warren took her hand. "He's fine."

"The important thing is . . ."

". . . He knows we love him."

By now, she was seated on Warren's lap. She gazed tenderly at his dear face. He ran his hands down her shoulders and arms, but she was too tired to respond. Instead, she rose and tightened the belt on her robe.

"You're right," she said. "We just have to get through this stage."

The next few weeks Teresa had a hard time keeping Flora's story from infiltrating her mind at inopportune moments. For instance, she thought about Flora learning of her mother's rape after she and Warren made love. Snatches of Flora teased her brain when she thought about Otto. She missed a whole sermon one Sunday thinking about her last teatime with Flora. Flora had the tea and cookies on the table when she arrived. They scarcely talked about the auction at all before Flora launched into the lucky part of her story.

The first day of junior high, Flora could hardly sit still, so great was her anticipation for art class. First period after lunch, she flew into the art room. Her stomach churned, and she could barely breathe. Her hands were clammy. The teacher—Mr. Faraday—had blond hair and long, elegant fingers. He wore horn-rimmed glasses that he pushed up on his nose with his forefinger. This was his first school.

Mr. Faraday handed out scissors, paste, and construction paper. Then he drew a pattern on the blackboard of a tulip bouquet in a squat vase. "This is what we're going to make today." He said some more things about color and design, but Flora didn't hear him. Cut and paste? Like kindergartners? She burst into tears.

Mr. Faraday got the class going before he stood over her desk. "What's the matter with you?" He sounded like a toy wound too tight.

"I came here to do art. This isn't art."

She saw him fist his right hand. He looked around at the class, busy cutting their floral patterns. He stooped low and growled in her ear. "Just what do you think you want to do?"

She sniveled. Wiped her nose on her sleeve. "I want to draw."

Mr. Faraday walked away, his steps fast and drumming. Hard-soled shoes on a hardwood floor. He rummaged around in a cabinet. He marched back, slapped a piece of paper on her desk, leaned over, and hissed, "Okay. You want to draw? Draw."

He left her alone the rest of the period. She took a pencil out of her backpack and drew a horse. She made the horse sassy and spry, mane flying. She paid attention to the muscles flexing under the horse's skin. She worked hard on the light in the eyes so you could tell the personality, defiant and bold. At the end of the hour, Mr. Faraday came and picked up her paper. He looked at her drawing a long time. Then he looked at her. The bell rang, and still he never said a word. She went to her next class and that night cried herself to sleep.

The next day, when the students were seated in Mr. Faraday's class, he held up the remnants of the cut–and-paste project from the day before. "This," he said, "is not art."

Flora felt her breath catch in a sharp uptake. She glanced around to see if any of the other kids were looking at her, but they only stared at Mr. Faraday. He picked up a trash can. The leaves and petals pinged against the metal as they floated down. Then he waved a large bound notebook. "This is the proposed art curriculum for seventh grade." That hit the trash can with a loud thump. "In this class, we will do art. Today, we'll start with drawing."

At this point in Flora's story, Teresa had a sudden and overwhelming urge to cry. Thinking of it in church on Sunday, she had to take out a tissue and blow her nose. Warren put his hand over hers. Otto had not come home until 2:00 a.m. the night before, and when he had come home, he'd been drunk. Even now, he was home sleeping it off. Warren thought she was crying about Otto, and Teresa let him think it. Maybe she was and maybe she wasn't; she could hardly tell anymore.

The first week in August, Otto was caught breaking and entering. He was a minor, so technically the arrest had some other name, but he and Quentin had been nabbed red-handed breaking into Ed Lambert's house. They broke a window when Ed was home, loading shells in his basement. They were damn lucky Ed didn't shoot them. Everybody knew Ed was crazy, and he was fed up with kids breaking in. This was the third time in a month, though Otto hadn't been involved before. After money, rumored to be hidden under Ed's mattress. Or maybe drugs.

"Drugs?" Teresa said, dumbfounded. She stood in the sheriff's office, one hand clamped around Otto's arm. Warren was in Hay Springs, working an auction.

She took Otto home. She had no idea what would happen to him. Something about juvenile court and being sentenced. The sheriff said Ed was considering whether to press charges.

She walked into the house ahead of Otto and sat in the kitchen chair and stared at the table.

Otto slumped in the doorway. He looked scared. She wanted to put her arms around him. Instead, she stood. "Are you hungry?"

He shook his head.

"Could you . . . Go to your room, Otto."

She reached under the sink and dragged out a bag of potatoes. She peeled six in long thin strips, forgetting there were only two of them. She sliced them with onions into a frying pan. Salt and pepper, turned them often. She dumped a mound onto a plate and took it to Otto's bedroom door, but she couldn't bring herself to open the door. She couldn't say his name. She couldn't knock. Finally, she set the steaming plate on the floor and went back to the kitchen. She picked up the frying pan, went outside, and dumped the contents onto the compost pile beside the garden. Looking at the browned crisp potatoes, the golden onions slithering atop a mass of decaying vegetables, she started to cry and knew she wouldn't stop anytime soon.

The day of Flora's sale dawned bright and sunny. Warren had a flatbed truck hauled onto the adjacent empty lot, and the best of what Flora had to offer was loaded onto the truck. An old violin. A set of Delft china. Waterford crystal candleholders. A couple of young men Warren had hired carried the furniture out to the front lawn. Otto used to help them, but he spent his Saturdays now working for Ed Lambert, doing whatever Ed told him to, mucking out stalls, digging holes that he filled in by nightfall. In exchange, Ed had agreed not to press charges. When he was not working for Ed, he was at football practice, the grunts and team yells reverberating across the field. Quentin was gone. His parents, too. No one knew where. Miraculously, Teresa's family had held together. They were intact. They were polite and careful. No one had time for movies. She and Warren hadn't made love since Otto's arrest. Really, everything had turned out fine. Just, sometimes Teresa thought the air in the house was tinged blue. When she looked at her son, she longed for a glimpse of the old Otto, her buoyant boy, and then she'd have to put her hand over her chest to keep from doubling over.

The rest of Flora's household goods were lined up on cardboard flats, stretching from one end of the yard to the next. Minutes before the sale, Warren would show up and group several of these flats together. People would have to bid on the lot, haul everything away. That was the secret of an auction—make the buyers feel they were getting a bargain and get rid of stuff for the seller. The crowd for the auction was small, but respectable. The usuals were there: old man McFlinty with his gray straggly beard hanging to the waist of his bib overalls; Tripper Washburn, whose nasal voice carried above everybody's including Warren's, even when Warren used the PA system; a few children playing tag around the decaying elms. One guy had driven an hour and a half to look at the old violin. He repaired instruments and wanted the curved wood from the sides.

The iron lung and all of Flora's personal belongings had already been trucked to Denver. Teresa had helped Flora crate and ship her paintings. They'd driven to Scottsbluff rather than to excite the curiosity of the Reach postal workers. Nobody knew a thing about Flora's fame or her troubled past or how art had saved her.

Flora was gone, too, choosing to move to Denver before the auction took place. Teresa walked through the empty house hoping to catch a glimpse of Flora, a whiff of perfume, a glance in the closet mirror. When the dining room table sold, Teresa longed to put her face to the wood, inhale deeply one last time, imprint her lips on the oak boards.

Finally the only thing left in the house was the old upright piano. Warren had the guys move it onto the front porch, but it was too heavy to carry down the steps. Once a player piano, the roller mechanism was broken. Warren tried to auction it from the stoop. Teresa stood in the crowd to help Warren spot any anxious bidder. Warren started at $20, but no one bid. At $10, Teresa noticed a boy, eleven or twelve, tugging on his mother's sleeve. From a few yards away, she could see that he was begging his mother to buy that piano. Teresa moved in closer.

Teresa didn't recognize the pair of them. The mother looked tired, haggard. She was middle-aged, middle-sized. Nothing remarkable about her. The boy was scrawny. He had a hungry look. Each time the boy stamped his foot and said, "Please," the mother shook her head. Teresa's heart pounded in her chest.

"Can I help?" She looked at the boy.

The boy ignored her. "Please, Mom."

"We already have a piano." His mother sounded weary.

"It's in the room with the TV. I can't practice when I want to."

"Where would we put it?"

"In my room."

"Do you play?" Teresa asked.

The boy nodded.

"If it helps," Teresa smiled at the mother, "I'm pretty sure he could have the piano."

"Stay out of this." The mother's voice landed hard and flat.

"See, Mom. It wouldn't cost anything."

The boy jumped up and down in his excitement. What was the matter with his mother? Couldn't she see her son? Standing right in front of her, couldn't she see him? He needed that piano. He was that kind of boy. Teresa felt an overwhelming urge to slap his mother. She'd never felt such hatred for anyone in her life.

"What would it hurt?" Teresa tried to keep her voice modulated and level. People had grown quiet around them.

The mother, embarrassed, leaned closer to her son. "How would we get it?"

"Dad. In his pickup."

"He can't manage that thing by himself."

"If you arranged a time, we could have some men here to help you." Teresa offered this in her kindest tone. She meant it. A gift to them. To this boy.

The mother turned on her. "Yeah? And what about at our house?

They gonna follow us forty-three miles up into the Sandhills to help unload it. C'mon." She yanked on her son's arm.

The boy looked stricken. He turned his pleading face to Teresa. His disappointment was electric, searing. All of who he was and wanted to become was tied to that piano. Without it, who would he be? Just another kid. Another normal kid. She closed her eyes. When she opened them, the mother and the boy were walking away, the boy's shoulders hunched, his spirit drained out of him, and Teresa did the only thing she could. She let him go.

MEN OF STEEL

A bad thing happened on the first day of Conrad's job that he can't talk about. Not that he's a big talker. He's from a family of reticent men, bred on the Nebraska prairie where topics range about as far as the weather and Cornhusker football. His uncle Gary served in Vietnam, his grandfather slogged through mud in France, but they don't speak of combat. Now Conrad knows why. Even if he could bring himself to talk about it, which he mostly can't, some of it's classified. His own momma has no idea what he's doing out in that godforsaken desert.

Conrad's a sensor operator. His job is to control the drone's camera and hold the guiding laser on target. He's seen death close-up before. On his uncle's farm they butchered cattle and hogs, wrung the necks of chickens and flung them into the yard where they danced, bloody and headless. He's tracked and shot deer, waited in a blind for a flock of ducks, blasted two pheasants with one blow from a shotgun. He tries to think of his job as an elaborate hunt: the hours of surveillance, the tracking, then the decision, and the kill.

He arrived at the base last May, his first day on the job Memorial Day. Nothing that bad has happened since, though he's seen some tough stuff.

He takes a lot of showers.

Home on leave, Conrad wakes in his old room. From his position on the bed he surveys his past—the statuette of him playing quarterback, the National Honor Society cord draped over the closet doorknob, Nancy Harmer's senior picture tucked in the side of the dresser mirror. Nancy's a student now at CU. She thought he made a dumb choice, going to the Air Force instead of college. For a while, she e-mailed, girlie stuff about parties and drinking on campus. He got so he wouldn't open her e-mails for two, three days. He liked the fact that a pretty girl wrote him, but the sight of her name in his inbox exhausted him. He quit writing, to be fair to her. Last night, after touching him too much and insisting he eat second helpings of meat loaf, his mother told him Nancy's studying in Italy this term. No chance of running into her. His mother's voice dripped sorrow, her hand scrubbing the back of his neck. He jerked away, saw the hurt in his mother's eyes, but what's he supposed to do about it?

He'd flown from Las Vegas to Denver, then boarded a tin can with wings that rocked through turbulent air to Scottsbluff, where his folks met him. They looked small. Older than he remembered. His mother cried. His dad shook his hand, full arm extended. During the drive to Reach, his mother's voice rattled like cottonwood leaves. He forced himself to listen. Between the recession and the Walmart going in at Scottsbluff, the hardware store is barely surviving. No shortage of sick and dying at the hospital, so at least her job's intact. They held back to let him enter the house first. In his hurry to get it over with, he stumbled on the threshold and nearly pitched to his knees. The house seemed different, though nothing has changed. Same beige carpet. Clorox and bacon grease. His mother's quilts and needlework crowding every wall. His dad barely visible.

He swings his feet to the floor, props his head in his hands. What day? Thanksgiving. Christ. He's not ready for this.

On the drive out to the home place, his mother fills him in on who's around this year: Uncle Bill, the family loser; Bill's daughter, Amalee, her husband, Terry, and their three boys; Aunt Irene, the token liberal, and her husband, who drinks too much; his uncle Gary and his wife, Laynie. The home place is theirs now. They never had kids, so there's tension around who will inherit the farm. Amalee could care less. Irene's three kids all live far away, propelled by college educations into city life. Conrad's the obvious choice, after all the work he's done. He shadowed his uncle so much that people mistook him for Gary's son. Conrad doesn't want the farm. He assumes Gary must know. The subject has never come up.

"What about Granddad?" Conrad asks. Though his father is driving, Conrad keeps his eyes on the road, sweeps side to side, scans the ditches.

"Irene's stopping by the nursing home. If it's a good day, they'll bring him on out."

They crowd into the farmhouse kitchen. Hugs, kisses, pats on the back. The air, warm and moist, redolent with butter, celery, and onions from Laynie's bread stuffing. His mother deposits three pies on the counter: apple, pumpkin, and cherry. Atop the cherry pie, his favorite, granulated sugar sparkles in the fluorescent light. Plump, bloodred cherries peek through the lattice crust. At the sight of those cherries, sour bile climbs up Conrad's esophagus. He swallows, grits his teeth, and turns away. Idiot. Wimp. No matter how much disgust he heaps on himself, he can't convince his stomach to stop churning.

His dad and Irene's husband escape to the den, where they will plant themselves in front of football and nurse bottles of beer, the requisite role for in-laws in this, his mother's family. Uncle Bill's wife is long gone, the result of his failed rock-star lifestyle, drunken and wild after his garage band failed to make it big following a performance on American Bandstand. As for Laynie, her being foreign has insulated her from the weight of expectation. If she's different, it's to be expected, and his mother and Irene can feel good about themselves for tolerating the stranger in their midst.

"Go on now," Laynie says. "Grab a beer, if you want. Gary and Bill are in the living room with Granddad."

Conrad studies her, to parse out whether she's changed or if she knows about Gary. Conrad's half in love with her. He can't help himself. He used to crane his neck to get a glimpse of her hanging wash on the line or bending over a flower patch. She came from Greece one summer to visit relatives. Gary saw her at a dance at the Legion Hall, wooed her behind a haystack, married her three months later. Besides dark smoldering eyes, Laynie retains a small accent. A mole sits above her upper lip, and Conrad has ridden through spasms of guilty pleasure centered on her mouth, her lips, and that mole. He'd die before he'd speak of any of this.

She looks straight at him, into him, and through him. She cups his face with her hand, small and rough from outside labor. "So sweet." Her voice, low and husky, moves him. Conscious of her breath, her perfume, he wishes he had the nerve to kiss her, even on the cheek. His face glows hot, and he ducks his head, fast, into the open refrigerator.

He comes up with a beer, and before he can twist off the cap, Laynie has turned away to give orders to his mom and Irene. He sniffs, wipes his nose on his shirt cuff, heads to the living room where he can hear nothing but the crackling of wood burning in the pot-bellied stove.

Gary and Bill, the dutiful and prodigal sons, are folded deep into overstuffed chairs on opposite sides of his grandfather's wheel-chair. Clenching bottles of Bud Light and staring into the fire, they could be a tableau for a beer commercial, except Granddad is not playing his part. Once able to outdrink, outshoot, and outcuss any man in the panhandle, he sits with one hand gripping the arm of the chair. The other massages his forehead, gouging at it with ragged fingernails, his forehead pitted with scabs.

Conrad sees the room as if it were a curio cabinet. Artifacts hint at a civilization he once knew but has forgotten: on one wall, an aerial photograph of the farm taken sixty-odd years ago, before indoor plumbing and before the windbreaks turned gray with dying elm trees; oak floors, stained dark; an oval braided rug hiding a bloodstain from the accident that nearly severed his granddad's foot; the walls, once green, mottled and faded like a day-old bruise; his grandmother's treadle sewing machine; an oil lamp rigged for electricity atop a white crocheted doily; a gliding rocker with a quilted throw tossed over the back, made by Conrad's mother: a roll top desk, cubicles stuffed with papers; shaggy lace curtains, tied back to let in daylight; a worn leather love seat joining the two deep chairs to form an arc around the wood stove.

Conrad makes his way to the love seat. Floorboards creak under his feet. He's relieved to sit.

His uncles wave their beer bottles at him.

"Conrad," Bill says.

"Heard you'd be home," Gary says.

Conrad looks at the floor between his feet. Swallows. Gary has not written one word. Not that he expected it. Not after the way they left things between them. Laynie e-mails and tells him what's happening on the farm. He writes his mother and Laynie, cheerful, mindless stuff about how pretty the desert looks in the morning. Sunrises and cactus, wide-bladed yucca, different from the soapweed back home. Shit he knows they want to hear. Nothing about death on the screen. Nothing real.

"Hey, Granddad." Conrad lifts his head. Hard to believe he was once afraid of this dried-up husk of a man.

"Is he ours?" The old man stares at him.

Conrad wets his lips. It's hot in this room.

"Don't mind him." Bill knocks his bottle against Conrad's knee. "He don't know me half the time, and I see him every week."

"Kathleen's boy," Gary says. "Conrad."

"C'mere." The old man waves one wobbly hand at Conrad. Conrad looks at Gary, uncertain. Then he drops to one knee in front of the wheelchair. The old man studies his face.

"If you're Conrad, you sure have changed."

Conrad looks at Bill and Gary. Both heads are turned away. He stands, uncertain what to do with his hands. He remembers then that he's holding a bottle of beer. He clanks it against Bill's, a mock toast of whatever the hell they want. Then he sits and gets busy drinking.

Amalee, Terry, and their boys arrive late morning. They blast into the living room. Everybody stands, except Granddad. The two younger boys, Troy and David, take off for the basement where Gary's set up the train table and the ancient Lionel with attendant tracks and station house and plastic people.

"You boys, we'll be having dinner soon," Irene shouts after them.

"Oh, let 'em go," Amalee says. "Let 'em run the stink off."

Amalee gives Conrad a quick A-frame hug. A Go Big Red sweatshirt and gray sweat pants camouflage her heavy body. She's still got that wavy blond hair. She barely acknowledges her father, but that's old news. Terry, a farm implement salesman, runs his hand over close-cropped black hair, wipes a residue of gel on his pants. Terry tries, too hard, to be everybody's friend and the world's best father, especially to his stepson Nick, a product of Amalee's teen pregnancy that once scandalized the town. Nick must be fifteen, sixteen now. He's slight of build, quiet, suffers from teen acne. Conrad watches Nick fidget and tries to send him a silent message: Don't worry. One day you'll outgrow the acne and this place.

Terry's all fired up, his voice banging off the walls. Amalee tries to shush him. Nick hangs back, hands in his pockets. Terry pulls Nick forward, pounds him on the back.

"First time he's got his own permit, this kid shoots a five-point buck. I tell you, it was something."

The whole group murmurs, except Irene. Conrad notices her disapproving silence.

"Go on, Nick," Terry prods. "Tell them about it."

"Naw. I don't wanna."

"Well, I'll tell it. I'm proud of you, son."

Nick winces. Conrad wants to pitch a tent over him, shield him from this public glare. Terry plunges on. "Amalee, go out to the car and bring in them pictures."

Amalee rolls her eyes but heads out the door. The group edges toward Granddad and the wood-burning stove.

Granddad raises glassy eyes, casts about for something familiar. When he catches sight of Gary, he hollers, "What did he say?"

"Nick shot himself a deer yesterday," Gary says, leaning over to put his mouth close to his dad's ear.

"Shot himself?"

"A deer. Nick shot a deer."

"Which one is Nick?" the old man yells.

While Gary tries to pacify his father, Amalee returns with the photos and Terry passes them around.

"Over on the old Sherbourne place. We went out early. Damn, it was cold. Nicky took off through that stand of trees down by the river. We walked, I don't know, thirty, forty-five minutes. I could see Nicky, he was maybe twenty yards away—would you say, Nick, about twenty yards?" Nick doesn't answer, busy studying his shoes. "I seen him raise his rifle, point at this big, beautiful buck standing in a thicket, just his head and big antlers sprouting up. Nicky got off a clean shot, downed him. Just like that."

Terry's story drones on like background noise to Conrad, who is riveted to one of the photos. The buck lies on the ground, his head twisted because of the antlers. Nick's on one knee beside the deer, his rifle nowhere in sight, his face turned forty-five degrees away from the camera. The deer and the boy mirror each other, their bodies awkward and pained.

Later, Conrad's smoking on the back stoop of the house. He needed some air and some space. The cigarette is just an excuse. He rolled it himself, carries the makings in his shirt pocket. He likes the ritual, the smell of tobacco, his tongue wetting the paper. He hardly raises it to his lips. He's thinking about Nick and that deer, both frozen in transitions neither of them chose, the boy galloping into adulthood, the deer heading toward oblivion and death. His Granddad, too, marching toward the grave. All of them, for that matter. They just don't know the details. He thinks about stuff like this a lot, stuff nobody ever talks about. He doesn't know if anybody else thinks like he does. He suspects they do, but sometimes he worries that there's something wrong with him, that he's morbid or strange.

He's out there by himself maybe ten minutes when the back door opens. Gary steps out, shrugs into a jacket.

"Mind some company?" he says.

"Suit yourself."

They stand silently for a while. Conrad studies the way the sunlight slices around the old windmill. Gary clears his throat. Conrad knows he's got something to say that's hard for him. He won't help him say it.

"It's over. Between me and that woman."

That woman. Conrad wonders what her name was. All he saw was her naked legs wrapped around Gary's waist, Gary standing bare-assed with his pants around his ankles, the two of them leaned up against a chest freezer on her back porch. Even now, he shakes his head to get rid of the image.

"She went back to Texas."

Conrad takes a slow draw on his cigarette, stifles a cough. "That the only reason?"

Gary doesn't speak. He's coiled tight, and Conrad waits. Then Gary says, "You had no business following me."

Conrad grunts, a bitter rueful sound. "We gonna have this fight all over again?"

Conrad pitches his cigarette butt into the yard. Most days, he wishes to hell he hadn't let his curiosity get the best of him. When he set out after Gary in that old pickup, wondering where Gary slipped off to mid-afternoon when he thought Conrad wouldn't notice, he never expected to find him shagging another woman. He would've bloodied the nose of anyone who spread such a farfetched rumor.

"I'm sorry for it, if that's what you need to hear," Gary says.

Conrad lets a beat go by. He's conscious of Gary leaning on the railing, breathing hard. He's shocked to discover that Gary's getting old.

"Does Laynie know?" Conrad asks.

"No. I didn't see no point in telling her."

So, that's what this is. He wants to make sure Conrad will keep his dirty secret. He considers letting Gary twist in the wind, but he can't do it. "Good," he says.

He looks at Gary. Gary nods. Both of them turn their attention back to the yard, as if all the answers to life's hard questions are spread out there on the hardscrabble dirt.

"You doing okay?" Gary asks.

Conrad swallows the gravel in his throat. He aches to tell Gary about that Memorial Day debacle. There was a time, before, when he would have been able to. He would have unburdened himself and believed that Gary was the kind of man so steeped in decency that he could absorb it.

"Yeah," Conrad lies. "I'm doing fine."

Later, at the dinner table, after they've had their fill of dressing and cranberries (Conrad skipped the bloodred cranberries), turkey and gravy, while they're enjoying a lull before the pie is served up, the talk turns to football. The Cornhuskers are not having a good year. They flail the coach for a while. Conrad says nothing. He's watching Laynie and Gary. She doesn't touch him when she walks by with a pitcher of water. She used to trail her fingers alongside Gary's arm, brush against him when she passed. He has to be asked twice before he realizes Irene is talking to him.

"Conrad, did you watch that game with Colorado?"

"No. I don't get much time for football," Conrad says.

"Not this again," Irene's husband mutters.

No one pays attention, except Granddad, who leans to Gary and shouts, "What did he say?"

Gary tries to dismiss the muttered comment, but Granddad tugs at his sleeve. Finally, Gary yells back, "Nothing, Pop."

"Nobody tells me anything." Granddad pokes at dribbled cranberries on his shirt.

Irene stays with Conrad. "There was a fight. Between one of our boys and a kid on their team. They'd been haranguing each other all day, one of them took a swing . . ."

"The other kid started it." This from Terry, who knows everything.

Irene glares at Terry. "They both took a swing, and they were kicked out of the game."

"As they should be," Conrad's mother says.

Conrad wonders where this is going. He notices Nick squirming in his chair, flinging green beans into the volcano of his mashed potatoes. Irene's gunning for something. Or someone.

"They awarded the Colorado kid the Chevrolet Player of the Game. After getting kicked out for fighting."

"He saved the game for the Buffs. If he hadn't made that end zone catch in the first half, they'd never have won," Terry says.

"I don't care." Irene's got her teacher voice on, judging and righteous. "What kind of message does that send? It's the same old thing. Wink-wink. Violence has no consequences."

"It's just a game," Conrad says. He's seen the consequences of real violence, eighteen inches away on a computer screen.

"No, it isn't, Conrad. You of all people should know that."

"What's that supposed to mean, Irene?" His mother, her voice strident.

"You know very well what I'm saying."

"I'm afraid I do," his mother says.

"We all do." Terry's tone suggests they've heard it a million times before.

Irene cranks up the intensity. "Guns, condoned violence, war. They're all of a piece."

At that, several start shouting. Conrad hears his own name. The word "sacrifice" shimmers out of the fray. Terry, foaming, spits out something vitriolic about Irene and armchairs, ending in "easy for you" and "kids who cop out." Conrad floats above, numb and unhurt, watching his mother's mouth open and close, watching Nick slip away from the table unnoticed, watching Gary watch Laynie, who does not look up from her plate.

"It's a damn shame we can't find some other way to resolve conflict," Irene says, getting the last word.

The whole table falls mute. Nobody looks at Conrad. His mind is on mucking out the barn, scraping up shit and hauling it outside. Backbreaking. He sees himself sweaty, the stench clinging to his skin. It occurs to him that they're waiting for him to say something. He opens his mouth and only one word falls out. "Shit."

He sees Irene redden; Terry suppresses a laugh. That's not what he meant. He tries again to explain. "Fuck."

He gathers his feet under him, every muscle straining to escape from this table. Before he can rise, Bill's hand grabs his elbow. Bill doesn't press, but he doesn't let go, either. Unless he wants to create an even bigger scene, Conrad has no choice but to stay seated.

"C'mon, now." Bill affects a strained laugh. "Am I gonna have to wait all day for a piece of Kathleen's pie?"

After dinner, the women head to the kitchen to do dishes, the men to the den for football. Conrad stands in the doorway to the den, leaning on the jamb. Through the window he sees the two younger boys shooting hoops by the barn. No sign of Nick, though no one seems concerned. He's probably sneaking a smoke or texting a friend about how awful his parents are. Conrad waits through the opening kickoff, then goes out to the kitchen.

Irene hands him a dish towel, gives his arm an extra pat without looking at him. No one mentions the dinner table. He dries and stacks plates on the table while Irene, his mother, and Amalee natter on about recipes and local people and Christmas plans. Laynie says little.

Finally, all that's left to put away are the big serving bowls that Laynie stores in the basement.

"Conrad, will you help me take these downstairs?" Laynie says.

"Need any more help?" Irene asks.

"Conrad and I can handle it. You three sit yourselves down in the living room. There's still coffee."

He grabs an armload of stacked bowls and follows Laynie down the steps. They walk through the finished part of the basement, past the train table, into the storage area. He hands Laynie bowls that she stacks into niches on the shelves. She doesn't speak. Neither does he. He moves to stand directly behind her, closes his eyes. She smells of lavender and sunlight.

She turns to him. One hand flutters at her neck, fusses with her collar. She reaches up and brushes a stray lock of heavy dark hair off her brow. He'd like to kiss the tiny crow's-feet springing from her eyes. His body's jazzed being this close to her.

"I know about the fight you and Gary had before you left," she says.

Conrad lets out a slow breath. He's not sure where to put his hands. They feel awkward and heavy hanging on the ends of his arms. The space is so cramped.

"I know," Laynie says. "I know about the affair."

Conrad's surprised, though he shouldn't be. The lack of touch. The tension between them.

"I'm sorry." She looks stricken and small. He fights the urge to put his arms around her.

"Yeah, everybody's sorry."

He stands, mute. What's he supposed to say?

"Anyway. I don't want you tiptoeing around us. Me."

"He doesn't think you know."

She shakes her head. Looks down. To the side. Anywhere but at him. Once, not that long ago, he'd dreamed of making her happy. Of being happy himself. He'd let himself think that if she found out, she'd let him take care of her. Now, she can't even look at him.

"You just going on like nothing's changed?" His anger is bigger than he meant to show, but it's outside him now, launched. There's nothing he can do to stop it.

"Oh, Conrad." She looks like she might cry. He raises both arms, grabs the shelves behind her, pins her body between his and the shelves. His breath heaves. She looks scared, and he wants to hit her to get rid of that look on her face.

"Don't cry." His grinds his teeth, speaks through a slotted mouth.

She shakes her head, eyes wide like a panicked doe. "No, I won't." Then, pulling herself more upright, she puts both hands on his arms and tugs them down to his sides. "You don't cry either," she says.

That makes him laugh, and he takes a step back. His breath evens out. Soon, he's miserable. "Sorry."

"It's okay." She wipes at her face with her hands, wipes her wet hands on her sleeves.

He runs one hand along his jaw, rough, behind his neck. His thoughts race around. It's hard work to tug them back to Laynie, but he does it. He finds the thread of their conversation and yanks on it.

"Why? Why let him get away with it?"

"At first, I wanted him to know I knew. To punish him."

"And now?"

She looks sideways, away from him. "I want us to be able to go on. If it gets called out between us, then we'll have to do something about it."

"It don't seem fair."

"I don't expect you to understand." She reaches out to him, places her flat hand on his chest. His heart cries out beneath her palm. "This will fade. All of this. Don't . . . don't stay mad at him, for my sake."

Conrad lifts her hand from his chest and kisses the inside palm. He leans into her until their foreheads touch. He feels her warm breath on his mouth, her hair on his cheek. He closes his eyes to dream of her and sees explosions, people running for cover, the desert, his life.

"I was younger, then," he says, his voice husky.

"Me, too," she whispers, and they stand that way a minute, maybe two, before she pulls away to head upstairs.

While Laynie joins the women in the living room, Conrad puts on his jacket and slips outside. He decides to take a stroll around the farm, revisit the old stone well, Laynie's garden, the barn where the two boys try to snare him into playing horse with them. He fends them off, walks down the lane to the machine shed. He runs his hand along the weathered siding. He's about to step around the other side to stride along the fencerow when he hears sniffling. He peers around the edge of the building. There's Nick, sprawled on the ground against the shed, face in his hands, shoulders heaving. He's crying full out, and Conrad quickly withdraws.

He slowly lowers himself until he's hunched against the shed wall, listens to the boy sob. He guesses it's the hunt, his first kill. Or Terry, a complete asshole. Maybe just being fifteen. Conrad squeezes his eyes, but the sounds of Nick's crying unnerve him. He shudders and tries to ignore the images crowding onto the screen of his mind. He trembles, and for a time, he doesn't know how long, he's not in charge of his present life.

Propped against the machine shed, Conrad waits for his pounding heart to quiet, the cold sweat on his brow to evaporate. He doesn't try to fight the nausea, just turns his head and spews his turkey dinner onto the ground. He wipes his mouth with the sleeve of his jacket and sits motionless. He stares straight ahead, steeling himself in case the images reappear. Nick is still crying, though quieter now. Conrad stays with him. On the far side of the machine shed, where Nick can't see him, he sits with the boy, because he doesn't want Nick to be alone. Because he doesn't want to be alone. Because, given all of this, it's the best he can do.

IN THE FLYOVER FICTION SERIES

To order or obtain more information on these or other University of Nebraska Press titles, visit nebraskapress.unl.edu.

OTHER WORKS BY
PAMELA CARTER JOERN

The Floor of the Sky (University of Nebraska Press, 2006)

The Plain Sense of Things (University of Nebraska Press, 2008)